Advance Praise for Animal Sanctuary

Sarah Falkner's *Animal Sanctuary* is a delicate and beautiful book. It is so perfectly structured, the language so carefully chosen, that upon being read it feels as though it takes place in the memory of the reader. While *Animal Sanctuary* maps the human world, it also maps the interstices of human and nonhuman animal interactions. Few books have successfully explored this space—Melville's *Moby Dick* comes to mind, and more recently Lydia Millet's *How the Dead Dream*. *Animal Sanctuary* is gorgeously different but it too successfully wanders here—and for this reason alone, it is a necessary book.

It is also a haunting book. Kitty Dawson still exists inside of me, and outside of me as well. She is in the world and I miss her.

— Jennifer Calkins, Evolutionary Biologist and Poet; Author, *A Story of Witchery*

I wish I had Sarah Falkner's mind as an academic curriculum. Her writing performs a kind of impossible alchemy by synthesizing primal experience, postmodern theory and political metaphor in narrative that is somehow beautiful, fluid and witty as it is enlightening.

— Cintra Wilson, Culture Critic/Author; Author, *A Massive Swelling: Celebrity Reexamined as a Grotesque, Crippling Disease*

Sarah Falkner

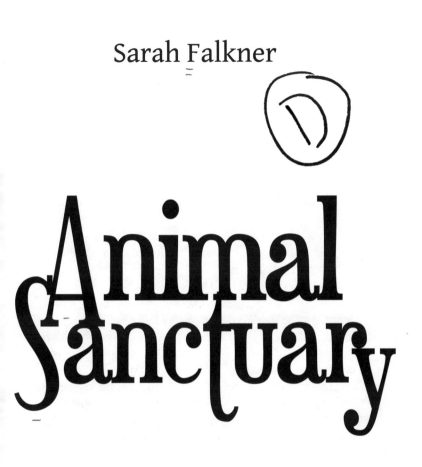

Animal Sanctuary

Fic
Falkner, S

Starcherone Books § Buffalo, NY

General Editor: Ted Pelton
Book Editor: Rebecca Maslen
Cover design: Julian Montague
Proofreading: Andrew Carrig, Emmett Haq, and Jason
    Pontillo

Cover photo: John Puslis, from the *Chicago Sun-Times*
    archive, Oct. 21, 1960. The location is the Lincoln Park
    Zoo, and the subject is Mrs. Helen Frederick, Director of
    the Lincoln Park Zoo. On the left a Barbary Lion, and on
    the right a Bengal Tiger.
Author photo on p. 221: Kahn & Selesnick

An excerpt from this book appeared in *Tatlin's Tower*.

Animal Sanctuary was chosen in a blind manuscript competition, with the selection from among five finalists made
by Stacey Levine in July-August, 2010. It is the seventh
book to win the Starcherone Prize for Innovative Fiction.

Library of Congress Cataloging-in-Publication Data

Falkner, Sarah.
Animal sanctuary / Sarah Falkner.
    p. cm.
A novel.
    ISBN 978-1-936873-09-8 (pbk. : alk. paper)
1. Actresses--Fiction. 2. Action and adventure films-
-Fiction. 3. Wildlife films--Fiction. 4. Mothers and sons-
-Fiction. 5. Animal sanctuaries--Fiction. 6. Human-animal
relationships--Fiction. 7. Animal welfare
--Fiction. I. Title.
    PS3606.A4287A55 2011
    813'.6--dc22

                                        2011030387

Personal Acknowledgments

I am especially grateful to Stacey Levine and Ted Pelton and feel
honored to have been chosen for publication by artists of such
caliber and integrity, and for whom I have so much
admiration and respect.

The support, encouragement, assistance and feedback of the
following people has been invaluable and essential:

Judith Blackstone
Jennifer Calkins
Jane Guskin
Nicholas Kahn
Loret and Michael Steinberg
J. Williams
Eric Wolske

Very special thanks are due to the residents and human staff of
the Exotic Feline Rescue Center in Center Point, Indiana.

I feel very fortunate to have received the excellent contributions
of Mela Ottaiano (editorial assistance); Ian Brewer (research
assistance); and Julian Montague (cover design).

This book is for Henry and Ivan most of all.

— Sarah Falkner

Contents

I   Some Films in Which Kitty Dawson Appears

1. Clouds gather and clot the clear blue expanse of the sky until it is thick and heavy and threatening to do something: what? As above, so below: a variety of dogs begin to appear in the streets, first singly, then doubly, then, if not already accompanied by a pack, joining up one already on patrol. Mutts nuzzle pedigreeds and mill in the alleys, phalanxes of hounds and shepherds assemble along chain-link fences, and tails of every color, length, and attitude thresh the air into an artificial breeze. So many pink tongues pant that what drips off becomes rivulets running to the gutters. People are not noticing, then wanting not to notice, then pretending not to notice as they hastily form their own alliances: first singly, then doubly, then running towards what feels safe, then just running. Some people do not run, paralyzed because they cannot believe what they are seeing, or they cannot understand why it is happening: and they each are overcome by the dogs, they are the first casualties. But then fall even some who run, and then succumb

even some who have taken shelter and fortified it: a bungalow has its doors and windows barred with the slats of dismantled crates nailed into the sills and frames, but the jaws and teeth deployed by the canine hordes are of such power and efficiency that when persistently applied they easily shred wood into splinters. You would think that old people, children, and the limping would suffer first and most in this situation, but logic seems to have been evacuated from the city, and so the weak gain some strange advantage they have never before enjoyed; the odds of survival are not what custom has previously dictated. In fact, the youthful and confident men seem to fall the hardest to the snapping jowls: sometimes, a single carefully-creased trouser leg terminating in a well-shined dress shoe is the locus of tug of war within a churning, furred patchwork lurching in every direction at once. You would think that the sound of hundreds, maybe thousands, of dogs barking, would not be so unfamiliar as to be discomfiting, but when it does not cease, after a time its crescendos and lulls begin to lap at the eardrum like waves of a storm-surge high-tide washing against sandbagged levees. A beautiful woman, blonde hair tidily arranged and topped with a sky-blue pillbox hat, runs through the streets in her high-heeled sandals and straight-skirted sky-blue suit; runs, though she does not understand exactly why she must. She takes shelter with an implausibly-bespectacled old woman, a truant child with pockets full of stolen candy, and a long-frocked priest: they sequester themselves within a department store signposted as out of business, condemned, and slated for demolition. Luckily the bankrupt merchants' creditors did not find profit in removing the dusty mannequins, and so as the old woman reclines with fear of heart attack, the blonde woman, the child and the priest make piles and heaps of abandoned plaster forms of humans, the stiff-fingered limbs stacking and interlacing like branches of underbrush gathered for a bonfire. These barricades seem even less sturdy than the wooden slats well-hammered over every egress that failed the residents of the bungalow, but nonetheless they manage to keep the dogs from entering the store through the revolving glass doors. A German Shepherd, a beagle, and a terrier-mix take turns hurling their bodies at the storefront window, each thudding impact different according to weight and velocity, until the glass cracks and a small passageway is afforded. But as the German Shepherd leaps with triumph through the jagged-edged aperture he is impaled on the shards, and the rest of the pack freezes. Instinct grabs the dogs by the scruffs of their necks as they sniff the blood of their own in the wind; they feel they've seen this kind of thing before. By the ancestral messages crucial for survival that have been encoded into their mitochondria, they are reminded that ranchers still warn coyote off grazing pastures by affixing some of their trembling brethren not yet dead of buckshot wounds to fence posts, by means of spikes; the dogs know in their bones that shepherds will garland the limbs of old oaks with the bloodied corpses of lamb-eating wolves. The dogs stop their barking, and run away. The people are heard weeping, and quieting, and weeping again as they realize they can hear themselves no longer drowned out by the incessant din of barking. Some time passes and the blonde woman, who has comported herself with dignity and grace throughout the horrifying events of the day, whose pillbox hat appears just askew enough to be a logical result of all her exertions, decides it is safe to peer out the doorway. The blonde woman finds a few people are beginning to creep out from their shelters: first singly, then doubly, then en masse. Strangers embrace one another and runny-nosed children are reunited with tearful mothers. The ones who survived cannot explain what happened, and do not care to try, once the general consensus is that it seems to be over.

2. A woman clad in a straight-skirted gray suit walks quickly enough to seem purposeful yet not so fast as to arouse suspicion in passersby. Her hair is a reddish-orange that does not occur in nature as human hair, but it nonetheless flatters her pale skin; she wears sunglasses and clutches a large black purse. A man with close-fitting black hair shiny from some sort of grooming product, who wears a suit of a darker gray than the woman's suit, is watching the woman and walking at varying paces, occasionally pausing to turn his head in the direction of a shop window or newspaper vending-machine, but all the while his eyes hold the woman steady, until she disappears into a shop readily identified even from a distance and at an odd angle by a cluster of three golden balls hanging above its door. The man waits for the woman to leave the shop and as soon as she turns the corner beyond it he enters the shop, and demands of the vendor,

"Sell me whatever the woman who just left has sold you!"

"Why, Mister, that won't come cheap," the old man replies, tugging at his anachronistic mustache and pulling from underneath the counter a small golden statue of a jaguar which, it will soon become evident, was found in the Yucatan by the man who, it will soon become evident, is named Mark. The next time the woman with reddish-orange hair appears she has blonde hair, and she is at a racetrack, leaning against a railing, watching with great interest horses that have just finished a race. Mark spots her through binoculars and approaches her, calling out "Lily! Lily!" which does not cause the blonde woman to look up. When Mark stands before the blonde woman there is a confrontation; she has done some things Mark does not understand. When they begin their conversation, the blonde woman makes many tiny rapid movements with her head and eyes and lips, flashing gestures of defiance and impatience, as if she were a racehorse and Mark were just the wind in her face trying to slow her down as she runs. As they keep talking, the blonde woman begins to look down more and more frequently, she has grown tired and no longer has the lead. The blonde woman, it turns out, is not really Lily, but Maria. Mark has deduced that the element of surprise is Maria's most-commonly used weapon and so he disarms her by feigning lack of shock at the sum and substance of her activities, adding that, all things considered, he still prefers the name he has come to call her, which is not just Lily, but Tiger Lily, and he adds, reaching out and coiling a ringlet of the blonde hair around his finger, isn't it true that tiger lilies are generally reddish in hue? The next time Maria appears, her hair has returned to reddish-orange. Mark and Maria each have things the other wants, though Mark seems to have more leverage in obtaining what he wants, and Maria seems like she might prefer to get what she wants from someone besides Mark. Maria has associates whose awkward, jerking gestures and ramshackle attire suggest trouble and unrest, they seem to have suffered much, and they also seem not always to care if others suffer, and it is uncertain how many of Maria's puzzling actions are out of empathy for these associates, or perhaps something else, like fear or loyalty or guilt. There is a man, Jorge, who wears an eyepatch that we are given to assume conceals an empty socket from which, the evidence implies, was ripped an eye by some general's henchman. There is a limping Josef. There is a smirking Costanza, who slaps Maria as if she thought such a gesture could keep her from escaping into a new life as Mark's wife. Though these associates of Maria and their hinted-at stories are compelling and fraught with danger and pain, we never learn too much about them; nothing matters as much as how much Mark wants Maria. Mark spends an awful lot of time following Maria and hiring people to find out about her past. He paces back and forth in his study, the shelves of which are lined with precious objects hewn of rock and smelted of gold for the elites of ancient blood-spilling empires, the walls of which are lined with the stuffed carcasses of brightly-colored birds and the decapitated heads of fierce beasts. It does appear that Mark is a man who collects things, who is accustomed to finding rare and unusual items, and keeping them. When Maria and Mark are together they bicker constantly, except when they are riding Mark's horses. They ride frequently. Eventually, after a jumping accident, Maria's horse has broken its leg beyond repair and must be shot to death. Maria grabs the pistol from Mark's hands and fires it herself. As the horse slumps to the ground, Mark embraces Maria, whose posture also sags, for she realizes that it is in fact herself she has just killed. Mark is more than happy to have what is still left of Maria, the part that just resembles her.

3.   A blonde woman stands on the sidewalk, pressed up against the cordons the police and firefighters have put in place to keep passersby from venturing into the black square of smoldering littered timbers that was a house. An arsonist is at large, and it is all anyone can talk about. As a reporter listens to a still-bathrobe-clad neighbor recount the sounds he'd heard the night before, his hair-rollered wife disputing each of his assertions with minor factual corrections, the reporter's hands are grasping a notebook and scribbling a pencil but his eyes are glancing more frequently at the blonde woman than they do at the notebook or the neighbor or the wife. Later the same night another house is burnt down, and the next day, another crowd stands on another sidewalk; the blonde woman stands among this crowd with her hands thrust into the pockets of her tan trench coat; also present is the reporter, who stands up straighter than usual and assumes a noble look as it dawns on him that now he is not just reporting on two house fires. In the days that follow, more houses burn, and the reporter eventually confronts the blonde woman, who he finds standing on every sidewalk found in front of every burnt-down house, and whose laconic manner and cryptic terse utterances

he finds fascinating. The reporter learns the blonde woman's identity, and searches some archives for information about her. He seems confused as to whether he wants to find something or nothing, but when he finds something he seems to have expected it all along. The reporter is the sort of man who is certain that a person who suffered a traumatic event in early childhood will become obsessed with that event the rest of his or her life, and must repeatedly reenact it in some fashion on one scale or another, and so the blonde woman's fate is at the mercy of the reporter who sets about convincing others that it is by logic such as his that the town must condemn the blonde woman for the crime of arson. The reporter seems confused as to whether he should help the blonde woman, or whether he should simply save the townspeople from more fires. He seems exhausted and sad as he picks up the telephone and asks to be connected to the chief of police. The blonde woman does not run when, in line at the bank, she overhears that she is wanted by the law. She chooses to go wait for whoever it is that might come for her at the art museum, where she sits on a bench viewing a painting of St. Joan atop a flaming pyre. At the police station, as an officer remands the blonde woman into the jailer's custody, another policeman arrives: one hand grappling a rough-looking youth in handcuffs and the other brandishing a metal gasoline can. The reporter is at their heels. The reporter lurches towards the blonde woman and blusters out the news that the rough-looking youth has been caught red-handed starting a fire and has confessed to the other fires, too. The reporter proffers an apology to the blonde woman, the substance of which is weighted most heavily towards making clear that, all things considered, it was only natural that he acted as he did, even though he didn't want to. The blonde woman remains sententious as ever, and the reporter grabs her and kisses her like it is a reward.

4.   A man enters an empty laboratory and steals a glass flask of what he thinks is an important vaccine that ought to belong to all of humanity, especially the disenfranchised that need it most. He returns to his tiny apartment where radical slogans are spray-painted directly on the walls, trash and books are strewn on the floor, and a pet white rabbit lopes freely throughout. The man telephones his co-conspirators and learns that, in fact, what he has stolen is something from an experiment with radiation and selective mutation, at a stage somewhere between live virus and cure. Abandoning whatever the original plan was, the man suddenly develops acute symptoms of a virulent avariciousness; he gets the idea to profit for himself, blackmailing the government into giving him money in exchange for returning the potentially-dangerous substance. As he mulls over, aloud to himself, various schemes that increasingly inflame his greed, his gaze grows distant and unfocused, and sweat beads his forehead. The rabbit jumps past him and knocks the vial to the floor, smashing the glass and spilling the contents; as the man curses and fumes, the rabbit scampers through the liquidy mess and hops out the open window. Miles away, a blonde woman is driving down a desert highway, and when a city appears in the distance she straightens up in her seat and proceeds forward, alertness possessing her face. Her eyes are fixed on the road but her mind's eye is trained on the city she approaches, and she imagines for herself the loved ones she once left behind there. She prays aloud but to no one in particular for forgiveness and a fresh start upon her return. Her dreams, and the car, come to a crashing halt as she swerves suddenly into the oncoming lane and the hood of her car crumples against a schoolbus. She turns her head towards what she veered away from, for it was really only the impression of movement seen out of the corner of her eye that startled her, and she'd like to get a better look; she catches a quick glimpse of a rabbit roughly the size of a buffalo, disappearing

into the brush. The entire accident was witnessed by a policeman who missed only one crucial detail: the rabbit. It is this
detail that threatens to completely nullify the blonde woman's
chances for a future; people she doesn't know are mocking, and
people she does know are disappointed and claim she still requires serious help and is too much a burden. As her time in
the city passes, the blonde woman remains friendless, jobless,
and completely unaware that a few other people have also had
similar run-ins with what will later be revealed to be giant, ge-
netically-mutated rabbits. The blonde woman walks into a bar.
Dim light casts shadows that reveal creases around her eyes
and mouth: she is not as young as she first appeared. It becomes completely understandable that she is utterly dejected
at having lost her chance at a fresh start, for how many others
will she have? It also seems the walk through the bar, from the
door to a stool at the bar, is much longer than it first appeared,
because in the time it takes the blonde woman to get to her seat
and order a drink—the imbibing of which we now extrapolate
would complete the final stage of her total downfall and return
to disgrace—throughout the city many, many other people are
running into trouble with giant rabbits. At last, enough people
who wield sufficient power and prestige that their perceptions
cannot be dismissed as madness or lies have seen the rabbits,
and the rabbits' existence becomes accepted as fact. As a news
report flashes on the television above the bar the blonde woman's story--and by extension, her reputation and sanity--is vin-
dicated just like that, just as her troublesome old companion
gin-and-tonic is handed to her. One strangely long and tenuous
moment has managed to redeem the blonde woman from having to take a sip from the glass, which she instead pushes along
the bar towards the slumped-over drunk to her right.

5. A young man and a young woman on their honeymoon accidentally learn some information the very knowledge of which

endangers their lives, and a number of volatile people falsely believe them to know even more than they do. The young couple runs through the back alleyways of colonial cities, bus terminals, and dilapidated airports hacked out of the jungle. They disguise themselves ineffectively, and they confound those who might help them by lacking any understanding of the language or customs of the country in which they find themselves. At last they find a sympathetic expatriate of their own nationality, an older blonde woman who runs a shabby, run-down bar in a backwater town, and though they only ever become briefly acquainted with one another, not only does the blonde woman save their lives and enable them to escape and return home, she even sacrifices her own life on their behalf, because with her age and experience, she knows it must come down to that. There are people with guns and there are dishonest government officials and there are large sums of money at stake, and the blonde woman sees that in a situation such as the one in which they all find themselves, a dramatic and preferably surprising development is required to change the probable outcome of the chain of events that have been set into motion. The blonde woman takes her time with death when it arrives in a storm of bullets and fire and men shouting, she greets this death as the best possible choice given the available options. She dies slowly and, once limp on the floor of her ransacked bar, makes certain that her face is soft and her limbs elegantly arranged, so that her last breath leaves a lovely pale figure in stark contrast to its immediate, desperate surroundings.

II BODY DOUBLE

It occurs to me, as I buckle my lapbelt and look through the scratched glass at the suitcases gliding and disappearing into the underbelly of the plane, that I am about to finish a grand and elongated migratory pattern: I am completing a lengthy cycle that begins and ends with flights. The first time I ever boarded an airplane, nearly eleven years ago, I made a flight that began my career: I was then what I would have described as a complete unknown, on her way to meet what she would have described as the famous motion-picture director Albert Wickwood, who had chosen her for the starring role of his next picture, having seen her in a local-television soap commercial while filming on location in a part of the country he described, in his autobiography, as a place having as its primary attraction a surfeit of desolate stretches of highway. I am now taking a flight that will end my career; the picture I am on my way to make will be my last.

1. It occurs to me that when I took my first flight it was still appropriate to dress as if for a formal occasion, and now all of the women on this airplane are bareheaded and wearing, as am I, pantsuits, or slacks, or even blue-jeans, or skirts—either so short or so long as to not seem much like skirts at all. These past eleven years so much has changed, some say the world has changed more in the past ten years than it has in any other ten years, and that sounds reasonable to me. Flying was, in the pill-box-hat-wearing days, a glamorous way to cross large expanses of land or sea, and I was, with great demonstrations of deference and solicitousness, reminded of that fact by those who made my arrangements for me; now flying is an economic mode of arriving far away, and there is no mention of any other options by those who make my arrangements for me.

2. It occurs to me as the jet taxies down the runway that I could now describe myself as the famous motion picture star Kitty Dawson, on her way to meet a director she had never heard of before her agent urged her to accept the role he'd found for her. The director of the film I am on my way to make is neither famous nor experienced, and though it is not his intention to end Kitty Dawson's career, and he in fact will give the film his best effort, the film will not be very good, will be at best forgotten soon after it is released, and Kitty Dawson's career will be finally and definitively over.

3. It occurs to me that Wickwood, the director who began my career and whose films were not just the first of Kitty Dawson's career but remained the highlights of it, in truth had tried his best also to be the director to end Kitty Dawson's career, not so long after he began it,

and that he failed at that must surely have pained him greatly.

It takes me four flights in all to reach my last film, each plane landing at an airport smaller than the one it departed from, each plane smaller than that which conveyed me for the leg of the journey preceding it, so that the entire journey, by the scale of its vessels and the paths they take, gradually telescopes down in size. The last craft that eventually alights on a slim patch of tarmac in a swatch of veldt is so tiny and lightweight buzzing above the tops of trees that I am no longer being transported by a giant machine like a jet but by something more like the storks wafting down to the edge of a watering hole we see during the drive to camp at dusk.

The makeup artist does not conceal her contempt for me as she wipes and daubs and scrubs and brushes-on. What causes her disgust? A flurry of dandruff, a line of dirt under a bitten-edged fingernail, enlarged pores on my nose all confirm that I don't stringently patrol the borders of my organism. I am completely remiss in all my required duties by the makeup artist's standards. The makeup artist scowls, unhappy with her work, making it clear her costly pigments don't cling as well they might on such an unprimed canvas as my face. She must be almost as surprised at my presence on the movie set as I am. Despite her antipathy I am tempted to tell her how it is I come to be here, for she is the only person who seems to notice I'm out of place, that an odd set of circumstances must have brought me here.

The plain of dried grasses to which I am brought the morning after I arrive is much brighter and hotter than it appeared in the photographs my agent showed me. The long days here near the girth of the globe that swells farthest towards the sun are vigorous bombardments by the sun's rays upon the vegetation and soil, and the planet's crust is so parched, bleached, and baked it can absorb no more heat and light and can only bounce it back into the atmosphere. I visited this continent once before, four years ago; we shot for a week in the country adjacent to this one, when it was known by another name; it was greener and cooler then and there. It was when I met Noel; he whisked me off on safari right after filming completed, selling, I later found out, one of his cars in order to raise the necessary funds on such short notice. I wish Noel were here with me now. He says he wishes he were here with me now, but insists he must take care of some business, secure us our future, though he is vague and loathe to give details. I worry less that he is busy with someone else than that he is busy with some scheme so risky and outlandish he feels he can't even talk about it to me.

Just as I arrive at the welcome tent Teddy den Hoven appears, and gushes:

"Kitty, you look lovely, delighted to meet you,"

as he mops his brow with a handkerchief in his left hand and grasps my right hand in his own. He looks past my face, over and beyond my right shoulder, as he catches sight of someone approaching, and before that person is in my line of vision he announces,

"Here's Catherine, she is your body double for all the animal scenes where we can't afford to risk your valuable hide, ha ha ha,"

he laughs as Catherine comes into view, and I see a woman whose hair is the same blonde as mine, who very much resembles what I looked like in pictures from eleven years ago.

> 1. Catherine is a crystalline, sharp-edged version of me; where I always soften, soften, soften my face, retreating from expressions that I have been told are less than flattering, are wrinkle-inducing, will eventually change

the structure of the face if held too firmly or frequent-ly, Catherine instead lets her features be sculpted and carved by various forces. Is it pride that lifts her cheek-bones so high, is it resolve that thrusts forward her jaw, what could lift her top lip in that remarkable line? I see some things in her face I'm too frightened to look for in my own when I see its reflection or reproduction.

2. Catherine makes no effort to flatter me, which I want to find refreshing but instead find makes my stom-ach hurt; when I realize she does not make any effort to flatter Teddy, either, I breathe a little easier. I learn Catherine will stand in for me when firearms are dis-charged, as she is about to do now, and when the lioness is set loose; she is not a trained stuntwoman and will not perform any remarkable feats or exertions, but sim-ply replacing my body with hers whenever possible in the presence of volatile situations with the potential for harm evidently greatly reduces insurance costs. No-one had set out to find such a person to take my place, but evidently the producer made Catherine's acquaintance by chance somehow, and seeing her close resemblance to me he thought it smart to take advantage of such an unusual coincidence; it does seem they can use all the money they can get or save for this production.

3. If only Catherine could stand in for me during the strangely equal-parts vague and specific scene that is meant to convey that my character is gang-raped, with-out changing the rating of the picture; a closeup of my contorted, anguished face cuts to the leering grins of my assailants with a soundtrack of ripping fabric, then a montage of hands grasping at wrists and ankles. If it were up to me I would rather risk gunpowder burns and

teeth and claws myself and have Catherine be the one to grimace and lay splayed out, but I know Kitty Dawson has been asked to make most of her pictures precisely because she would not ask the director to change a thing about how he wants to make the picture, and so I just look forward to seeing how it all turns out.

I realize I am watching Catherine blankly, waiting for her to speak, wishing she could somehow guess how I wish she would do the rape scene in my place and make the offer herself.

Poor Kitty! Her eyes are like a startled gazelle's as she realizes she's looked at my face for a very long time, as she realizes I have noticed. It is likely she has never before examined another woman's face with such a languorous, meandering pilgrimage to features of the landscape of the body such as desire, or in her case, recognition, leads us take.

"Kitty, is the heat affecting you?"

Teddy asks me, understandably, as I have stood a moment too long looking at Catherine, my face beginning to betray I'm thinking something I'm not saying.

"No, really, I'm fine."

How easily that phrase comes out of my mouth! I am shepherded toward a seat and a glass of cool water, but what most refreshes me is that there is a simple enough explanation for an awkwardness, and someone else has supplied it.

"No, really, I'm fine," says Kitty Dawson. NO REALLY I'M FINE read a telegram I received from Marina, six weeks ago, four words that immediately made my heart race, that made me sell my bicycle and books and borrow from friends to raise funds for a ticket over here.

Letters from Marina after she arrived here began as a biweekly event, becoming less frequent after the first two months, then quite erratic for another three months. Her sixth month here I received no letters. I tried to believe she had become tired of me, that the beacon of our connection to one another had dimmed, that my staying to finish my studies had in her mind metamorphosed into a cowardly desire to pass for a bourgeois college student and enjoy the privileges thereof. So when the telegram came I was momentarily relieved she still shared our coded language, while at the same time I was worried at how exactly she was not really fine.

1. When no one else was home but me and my father, he would come into my room, and he would grab hold of an arm, a leg, a hank of hair; he would grab hold and twist and pull and stretch, and he would arrange my clothing and bend my limbs in some fashion or another until some orifice or another dilated enough for him insert some part of his body or another inside it. One afternoon he is still arranging himself back in his trousers, his shirtsleeves still rolled up to the elbow, when there is a knock at the kitchen entrance and a schoolfriend calls out for me through the screen door. I am admonished to collect myself and go send her away politely, and he raises his hand, I hate him even at the same time as somehow believing he is actually doing me a favor by not bringing the back of his hand hard across my face as he well could, and he throws in for good measure, "And who said you could have a friend come to the house?" I speak to my friend veiled through the screen door, my words filtering through the mesh. How I long that the words I say would get trapped in the net of the screen so that what I can't say, what I'm thinking, a finer truer substance, might pass through instead. My friend persists in asking whether I am sure everything is alright.
"No really, I'm fine."

2. From time to time a couple of women are seen whispering to one another. Sometimes it is two mothers of schoolmates in the schoolyard, sometimes two teachers in the classroom, sometimes a woman at the door whispering to your mother. Sometimes there is crying and gesticulating, sometimes a low moaning sound and a worried looking around to see whether anyone is paying attention. Sometimes there is an empty desk in the classroom that no one will look at, sometimes the house down the block is suddenly boarded up, sometimes the neighbors from upstairs are never seen again. This is not spoken of, and one does not ask about it. One summer night Ines' Papa, who teaches at the University with Marina's Papa, is not at the dinner table. It is not commented upon; the girls are entreated to eat, bathe, go to sleep. The next day at school, Teacher calls Ines aside just after lunch recess. "How are you doing, little one," she asks very earnestly, her eyes searching Ines' face. Ines pauses. She is nine, and she is familiar with many tales where a person finds herself in a luxuriously-appointed castle where everything that a person could want is provided, so long as she doesn't open the little door at the top of the upmost tower, or ask why she can't. Ines and Marina love to read each other stories in which a little girl's wrong answer to a query from a hideous gnome met upon a woodland path can mean a shower of pitch falls upon her instead of gold coins raining from the sky as they did upon her cleverer sister who answered the gnome's riddle correctly. It is common in the world that people must endure all manner of puzzling circumstances and strange questions from strange beings, but if they conduct themselves well, ask and answer questions carefully, they triumph in the end, they are awarded riches and castles and fine horses, they even save the brother who has been baked by the hag into a pie and the parents chopped into pieces and thrown to the bottom of a well. So, Ines knows what she must say. Marina watches their teacher press Ines further: *"Are you sure?"*

"No really, I'm fine," Ines replies.

3. Pamela Hamilton in the hallway, on the other side of the door to the dormitory room Marina and I share, is not immediately satisfied with my plea of inability to move due to menstrual cramps. Pamela, having come to collect me on the way to the review session to which I'd agreed to accompany her, seems to understand I am not telling the truth. Pamela only likes my company slightly more than the thought of going alone to an event, and that she dreads; I care for Pamela's company about as much as I care for what the girls, the women, at this school think of me, and that concern is a rapidly evaporating substance. Inside the dormitory room with only the thin flat wood of the door separating us from Pamela, on Marina's bed we sprawl a doubled Venus, as in that painting we have seen in art history class: the painter's mistress draped like a length of costly brocade, looking into the full-length mirror an enterprising winged Cupid proffers so the painter's patron gets double for his money, so the viewer can see dimpled buttocks and a serpentine line of vertebrae in the same picture plane as a frontal tableau of polished-gem eyes, plump lips, berryish nipples, and the hairless harelipped crevice towards which all the lines of drapery and the mudra of Venus' tapered fingers gesture towards, a well-paved route even the most weary or drunken aesthete's eyes can make their way along. But it is no reflection or painting I gaze at now, I stare at another expanse of feminine skin stretched out alongside me, another pair of breasts facing my own, another tender-woolled cleft opposite mine. I cannot at the moment recollect how we began. We have spent the last few hours sharing our stories, surveying the maps of our histories, and erasing the regions of bruises with kisses, obliterating all traces of where fists and blunt objects once landed, where rough hands tried to stake their claims, where restraints once ensnared: we grew up in very different places, but it seems the terrain of our homelands bears striking similarities. And now we are both far from home. Here in our room I feel like two foxes who outran the hounds, outwitted the hunting party, and at last find themselves safe in a den, licking each other's wounds. But with the arrival of Pamela and only a thin door between us, I am reminded Marina and I are really only safe so long as no-one finds us here in our fox-form, we must shape-shift back when in the company of anyone else.

"Are you sure you don't need help?" Pamela persists asking through the door.

"No really, I'm fine."

I go to the national museum in the capital on my day off. Noel suggested that I come here, when we spoke on the telephone. I am meant to be playing a landowner, and I would like to learn more about the local history of farming, which cannot in this country—perhaps anywhere on this continent—much resemble the farming my father and uncles attempted. I know so little of the people here; four years ago when I was a hundred or so miles away filming *Peaceable Kingdom*, which has very few people in it, we only ever saw the animals. That is the part I most look forward to in this film, working with the lion cub and the lioness.

"We are glad you came today,"

they tell me at the desk,

"Yesterday, the power was cut most of the day! Mrs. Dawson would not like to walk through our museum with the lights and fans off!"

I am surprised to learn the museum is only about five years old, as already it seems weary; I wander past case after dusty glass case housing ceramics and woven items fashioned in methods used continuously for thousands of years. After so many pots and baskets, when I see the case in which a group of skulls are displayed they seem nestled on their shelf like any other group of traditional containers. One skull, that of a baboon, is presented upside-down with a cardboard placard of remarks at its side. The faint yellowy-tan interior of the cranial bowl is marked by the bones' meandering suture-lines, looking like glued seams of a clay pot assembled from shards. Dusted with a papery, powdery sheen indicating where something less durable than bone was once attached, this vessel's resemblance to an empty walnut shell mocks me as I pause and consider that for all I understand of its workings, the brain might as well be an oily nutmeat. After the shelf of skulls comes a case filled with animal skins, then some tall cases filled with knives and guns, and then some beribboned and bejeweled military uniforms, and cardboard placards listing year after year after year of campaigns, wars, battles, revolts: the names of the struggles and the years they took place. It strikes me that gazing at all this, I remain ignorant as to who died, how many died, who was on which side, who won, what really they were fighting for, any of them.

"Ma'am, please, this way,"

says a voice from behind me, the young shiny-faced curator they've found for me—Mr. Pivin, according to a nametag on his jacket lapel. Mr. Pivin's white shirt collar is starched so stiff it seems to have been removed on loan from the display of uniforms. Mr. Pivin walks backward so he can face me as he leads me towards cases of farming handtools and dried seedpods.

"We are modernizing rapidly now!"

Mr. Pivin exclaims, and nods his head. He gestures with both arms outstretched, indicating everything we have to look at and says, for the first time smiling,

"Soon, all this will disappear entirely!"

This movie, A Family's Pride, *is the most ridiculous story! It*

comes as no real surprise to me, but nonetheless to see firsthand the amount of time, effort, and money that is put into this and presumably any of the other filmic confections that they gobble up back home in such great abundance, no nutritive value, the flavor forgotten not long after, it makes me sick to my stomach as if I'd eaten poisoned candy myself. And to feast on such trifles when here all around us is so much suffering, wanting and hunger! But so many yawn when I speak of this, people back home; they know this all already, if they care, then they are of course already doing the best they can, but more often, what exactly has it got to do with them, and what can they do about it anyway? Everyone says that in the last decade so much has changed for the better, and that is true when you look at things a certain way, but at the same time, so much has not changed, and people seem to be becoming less concerned about achieving more change; now it seems good enough for many people that things appear or are said to be, different than they once were. Back home, for awhile it was as natural to take the streets, protesting and demanding change, as it was to go dancing on a Saturday night; now, it seems good enough for many people just to know that marches still go on even without them—though the marches get smaller and smaller, and the vibe has completely changed. Of the war, the president says the end is in sight—though I don't believe that about the war, I do wonder whether we have moved beyond something, towards an end of something, without really understanding what that something is. People I hitchhiked with to protests, people I went to meetings and teach-ins with, people who chanted in unison 'power to the people!' now they tell me they're evolving, they've realized how important it is to work more on themselves, to get more in touch with themselves, to find their "true selves"; they're changing their programming, changing themselves, and they're saying they've realized "true change" comes from within. I understand we have to change ourselves, too, but achieving this "true change" solely via self-help, contemplation, consciousness-raising, it doesn't seem like a fast enough method on its own when still, every day, lots and lots of people are dying all over the planet thanks to wars, famine, and other situations our government seems to have a direct hand in. I wonder if a mother watching her children's skin burnt away by the Agent Orange our tax dollars pay for thinks this "true change" method achieved one citizen at a time is a fast-enough way to get our government from spraying defoliant on the jungle that has housed and fed her family for tens of generations.

Well, who am I to talk about fast-enough methods, at the moment? Every day I'm here I have more insight into just how ill-prepared I was to visit this place, let alone accomplish anything like what I was hoping to accomplish here.

I am told that the culture and tourism commission here eagerly solicits film productions such as ours; the commission was specially-formed under the ministry of trade and industry as the members of the cabinet feel the movies are an industry that will improve the country's fortunes, create jobs and, that ineffable metamorphosis, modernize. Yesterday, the daily allotment of six hours of electrical power was cut in the capital—an unscheduled cut, as opposed to the very regularly scheduled blackouts and brownouts. Most of the capital's residents don't rely on the electricity that's so erratically supplied by the state, but they have become accustomed to running their generators; so the simultaneous liquid fuel shortage was what was most upsetting to the average person yesterday. But our movie, our neatly-contained encampment just outside the city, with its own generators running on a well-secured store of diesel fuel, was not interrupted for even an instant, our little world's inhabitants were not inconvenienced in the slightest and not even aware that a few miles away there were dimmed lights and machines lying idle, business of all manner was delayed, food was sold out of rapidly-warming refrigerators at non-profit prices, for want of some kind of power.

I understand now why, so shortly after meeting me during the layover in Frankfurt the producer was so insistent on taking me under his wing. I resented this middle-aged man's airport bar-induced paternalism almost as much as my own jetlagged acquiescence to it, but now what I resent the most is that by chance I resemble Kitty

Dawson, by chance the producer of a film starring Kitty Dawson was waiting for the same flight I was, by chance I uncharacteristically divulged to this man that I had little money and a missing friend in a place I knew little about, by chance he got an idea that would enable him to feel benevolent and noble—while saving his movie production some money—and so it is also by chance that in spite of myself, I have made it this far, and nothing horrible has happened to me yet. When I was ten years old, my dog Sasha slipped her leash and ran into the highway, and I immediately ran after her, barely hearing the blaring horns and screeching brakes: everything around me a complete blur except for Sasha's black and white form. So it is now that my eyes rarely focus as I scan every crowd, every street for the shape of Marina; and everything races all around and past me yet without serious impact—for all that, there is no explanation but dumb luck.

Marina was hardly much more prepared than I upon her arrival here; I understand now at least one reason why her letters slowed in frequency and then stopped. Before she left, the distance and difference were abstract; after our initial disagreements, we agreed that in spite of the distance that would be between us, we would remain feeling close, two halves of a single unit; while we were in two different locations engaged in two different tasks we were ultimately working toward the same goals, engaged in the same struggle. Upon arriving here, the concrete reality of this place and all its intricacies and details quickly erases the outlines we'd sketched when this place was just an abstraction figuring in our plans.

When I arrived at college for the first time there was a similar blotting out of all else save as much of the immediate chaos as I could take in. I was the first of my family to attend college and went with dreams that there I would be able to do good, make better: not just myself and my family, but anything to which I applied myself. I believed I would gain special skills and abilities that would enable me to contribute more than I could have otherwise, I tried to do my best at every moment and still always found myself lacking. Everywhere I looked in the world I saw urgently disastrous situations, and daunting as any one of them seemed, it struck me that surely what is human-made can be human-undone; surely what is human-made must be human-undone. But where to start, where to focus, were questions that plagued me night and day for months, and the more I learned the more complicated it seemed to get. I tried to assess the most urgent cause of all those that people around me were involved with, the one for which I might be best suited; I attended meetings and protests, I helped prepare and serve food, handed out flyers, asked passersby to sign petitions, skimped on sleep and food, contributed a greater percentage of my meager wage from the cafeteria than my more privileged classmates donated from their allowances. Yet, despite all this activity it never felt I was doing anything that mattered in a big enough way, and after awhile I felt a clock inside me counting out the time I'd wasted trying to figure out what it was I should be doing most of all instead of actually having done it. And then I heard Marina speak at a meeting. She told the story of Ines and her father, tears in her eyes: Ines had been her best friend when she was little, Marina and her family had lived in Ines' country when Marina's father had been part of a university physics faculty exchange.

Marina had a catalyzing, clarifying effect: when she spoke—whatever it was she spoke about—she seemed always to emphasize what was most important about something, what feelings, thoughts and actions could be organized around best. When she was at my side I could begin to see order and patterns I could recognize like a cityscape in the fog—the lurking silhouettes of major forces inventing, generating, and maintaining the causes of suffering: the factories and machinery of injustice, artificial structures that would need to be demolished. Together we studied and talked until not only could we both count the levels and stories and foundations of some of these structures, but also see how we were not alone, also see through the fog the strands of a web connecting us to each other, to others—connecting our desire to others', our suffering to others', our responsibility to others'. We began to see what seemed to matter most.

As our vision grew more acute, nothing became so clear as the

*fact that all of these structures—put in place so long ago and main-
tained for so long—would require even more enormous efforts to be
dismantled; it was best to get started, to plan for the long run. Together we decided I would remain at college, studying in the library
and laboratory things I had already both found myself with aptitudes
for and found to be useful for our causes, things like documenting the
effects of violence on the body, the effects of blunt force and psychological trauma on the central nervous system, I would catalogue the
effects of pain and hunger and want and suffering on the human organism; I would learn to assemble proof in the interest of convincing
other people, the people who need evidence and reason to inspire their
feelings and actions. I would assemble proof that it was important
and necessary and possible to take action, and I would demonstrate
what would happen if action were not taken.*

*Marina on the other hand couldn't bear any more proof, her en-
gines were so stoked with it she would explode if she didn't take off
soon in the direction of direct action, to a place with people in the
most urgent need. We agreed that while I stayed at college she would
leave it for something more active. But then she announced she'd
picked this place, where there was a staging ground for relief efforts
for the war two countries away, and it was then that we had our first
quarrel. I couldn't say exactly what it was that bothered me most, so I
offered what I could articulate at the time: we'd made other decisions
together, so why had she suddenly decided on her own what she was
going to do? I asked her why the struggle over here was any more important than the struggle on the next continent, let alone, the struggle
at home, where after all there was a war of a different sort on against
our own people; there were people in urgent need in all of these places,
weren't there, weren't they all related, why was it suddenly a contest,
how had she decided what cause was most worthy? Wasn't fighting
the roots of oppression where we were most effective going to help
resolve conflicts everywhere? I also admitted to her that I didn't want
her to leave me, that I did not see how that sacrifice would make our
work any more effective or meaningful.*

A week after Marina left, I read a quote—at the time attributed to an "anonymous Aborigine"—that seemed a lightning-strike whose bright flash revealed with both pain and utter clarity a concise remedy to all that had troubled me over the past year, all that troubled me about Marina's decision:

*"If you have come to 'help,' please go away. But if you have come because your liberation is bound up with mine, then let us walk together." ***

After reading this I immediately thought of Marina's friend Bennett's response when I'd asked if he and his girlfriend wanted to come with Marina and I to a report on the current situation in Chacahuatineja.

"I didn't even know there was some situation down there," he said.

"Great—like we didn't have enough places to help already!" sighed his girlfriend Eve, who had just applied for the Peace Corps.

Bennett, seeming as long as I'd known him to be preparing for the life of a young male pedagogue with lots of young female minds to educate, had corrected me several times in casual conversation, so I was not too eager to try to explain that the people of Chacahuatineja had successfully resisted their dubiously-elected president's various oppressive "reforms," through both active protest and demonstration, as well as the creation of alternate economies of barter and communal support. I thought we could learn a lot from the people of Chacahuatineja; I thought they could help us.

And so I was, in light of this "anonymous Aborigine" quote, also able to admit to myself why it had made me feel so strange when Marina had once introduced me to a friend as the "daughter of a feminist, a woman who chose to work even while she had young children!" I had been speechless at the time, realizing that Marina either could not or would not understand there was no choice in my mother's "decision" to pay the rent, put food on our table.

Now I can, and must, admit there was yet another reason I was suspicious of Marina's choosing to come here. It was because by this time I had heard her tell the story of Ines and her father a couple of times, in different settings, and while the story never failed to elicit emotional reactions in its listeners—usually our fellow students—certain details did not remain constant. Ines was Marina's best friend, then she was her cousin. Sometimes Marina was sleeping over the night of the disappearance, sometimes she learned about it the next day. Sometimes Marina continued to hear from Ines for a year after Marina's family returned home, sometimes Ines disappeared a week after her father. Sometimes Ines had one sister, sometimes two. I worried about how much of the story was true, even sometimes wondering if any of it was true. I began to feel myself like the possibly-mythical Ines, faced with a situation in which I might ask the wrong question and an enchantment would end. This story had given me, and perhaps others, purpose, energy, focus to do many things that were unquestionably of merit; what spell would unraveling this story undo, what else would I find if I pulled at the loose ends? Perhaps it was my fears about this that led me to give up struggling against her plans to leave.

I wonder whether the daughter of a middle-class university professor, albeit one with some sort of personal connection to another middle-class university professor presumed abducted and tortured to death by secret police in a country under fascist dictatorship, upon arrival here felt any more equipped to deal with this place than I do, any less bewildered by the overwhelming sense that here there is the potential for everything to go horribly, violently wrong.

Our studies at the university, Marina coming here, now me coming here: all of this because we wanted, needed, to help. It had all made sense at some point; and what more can we do besides try our best, we had said. That feeling of it all making sense, that trying our best is all we can do, that all seems to be left back home, seems perhaps only applicable back home.

> *1. Kitty Dawson's character in this movie, Karen Thorssen, is the lonely, dissolute heiress to a colonial plantation that has fallen into decline due to indolence and neglect by the Thorssen*

family that has dissipated and withered in a climate so different from their cold-stone, dark-wintered ancestral stronghold.
When the story opens, peacock-blue chiffon-caftaned Karen,
martini in one hand and cigarette in the other, blonde hair
bedraggling at the same rate the gin and vermouth are slosh-
ing about in the glass, is haggling with an itinerant merchant
in an attempt to get a higher price for some jewelry she is selling off. After the barest of character definition, the real story
begins: one of Karen's farmhands comes into possession of a
lion cub, said to be the daughter of a man-eating lioness killed
by the villagers, and when Karen—who seems never to have
previously shown interest in caring for any other creature,
least of all herself—learns of the cub's fated sale on the ille-
gal market, she impulsively demands that the farmhand turn
the cub over to her. Karen makes a project of raising the cub
and in the process improves herself: she is never again shown
drinking or smoking, she dons sensible clothes, takes an interest in the practical business of running the farm, gains the
admiration and friendship of the farmhands and villagers as
everyone's fortunes improve together. The raising of the cub
becomes the salvation of Karen; Karen's salvation is that of
the farm; and the farm's salvation that of the village. Though
the cub grows up sleeping on silk couches and cuddling with
Karen as they listen to concertos on the record player, when
the cub grows to be a certain size Karen has an epiphany and
decides that it is imperative that the grown cub be sent into
the wild, to live among other lions, free, independent; and
this act is first and foremost to be considered Karen's noble
sacrifice. Karen lets the lioness go at the farthest edge of the
farm. She tearfully confides to Nkisi, who once possessed the
cub and now as her right-hand man bears no visible grudge
towards Karen for her seizure of what he once considered his
property, that she fears the cub will become like the man-eating lioness-mother she lost so long ago; she cannot be certain

that despite having lived among humans who cared for her and provided her with luxuries and comforts the lioness will not revert to what Karen calls "her more primitive instincts." Karen's suffering transfigures her further, and she endures further suffering in the absence of the lioness—bandits raid the farm and set fire to its buildings, Karen herself is physically attacked—but Karen draws up her courage and rallies the villagers to band together and start over; Karen means to stay, even if it requires sacrifices and losses; and the villagers want her to stay, by now they need her! A montage indicates that months pass, we see that the farm has been rebuilt: and then the lioness reappears, with her own cub at her side, having attained what appears to be her natural state, yet not at the expense of friendly contact with humans.

2. The lioness and I are both doubles, stand-ins, mute representatives of others with more agency and language, our activities restricted to moving to marks as indicated.

3. Karen the character is a stand-in for the film director: he and his kind have for this country, the whole continent, and its people the same condescending fears, hopes, and appropriation Karen has for the lioness.

4. Perhaps I will watch this film when it is finished and I will eat some of the poison candy I so harshly judge others for eating. I will watch this film and the lioness will be a substitute for Marina, and I will pretend that it is reasonable to expect that a creature that disappears will come back.

5. Perhaps this country, for Marina, was a substitute for the place where she lost Ines, or idealized an Ines, or invented an Ines, or however it actually was: two places of vast grasslands and vanishing people. Perhaps Marina could not save what

and who she wanted, and so she applied herself to trying to save that which most resembled what or who she couldn't save. Perhaps Marina did not know what or who she wanted to help, how or why she could—should—be of service, and so she invented it. Perhaps Ines, the idea of Ines, the idea of saving a person like Ines, was a substitute which Marina preferred to what was more complicated, less dramatic a story, but ultimately really directly more her responsibility, those things close to home more within her reach, more within reach of attaining modest but meaningful results for the better.

An envelope arrives from Noel. It contains a photograph of our living room, and in the living room, on the green paisley couch, is a lion, a large male, with a full mane.

"Call me when you get this!" is scribbled on the back. And I do.

1. Here I was doubting Noel, feeling so far away from him, and all along he has been thinking of me first and foremost, taking action on my behalf, having my best interests in mind. I find he has decided to produce another film. He said before he had quit, but this time it's different; and it's for me, and with me in mind from the very beginning.

2. Here I was feeling a stranger to Noel, and he in fact knows me as well as I know myself. He understood how much I fell in love with the animals when we went on safari after *Peaceable Kingdom*; he has taken to heart how much I want to work with them, so much so that a couple of weeks ago as he was reading in a magazine at the dentist's how drug dealers and occultist types purchase lions and tigers thinking to make impressive pets of them and then they can't take care of them properly, there

are small circuses and places that go out of business and the animals don't get a new job or a second chance but instead just get destroyed, and so there are plenty of these big cats that need a good home, and reading all this Noel thought, why not make a place for these cats and make our own safari right here back home, on forty acres we can have both our own game park and our own film set; we couldn't afford to film on location, but now we won't even have to answer to anyone, we can do it our way! He hasn't gotten the land just yet but as the photograph shows he has already taken in Hector from a satanist who was having trouble affording the weekly bills for all that meat, which Noel has figured out how to pay for, for the time being.

3. If anyone can make this work, Noel can. Perhaps *A Family's Pride* is not to be my last film after all! Kitty Dawson is not yet down for the count!

The consulate informs me that people, foreigners, do disappear from time to time—especially if they travel outside the capital, especially if they are not escorted or affiliated with an appropriate organization, especially if they are engaged in activities the state department does not recommend its citizens abroad engage in. They convey their position that Marina seems to have been completely reckless, unqualified, naive, wrong in how she went about her mission, and certainly in conflict with their recommendations. They suggest that, generally, the young tend to romanticize situations that are best left to those with experience in such matters, that idealism clouds one's judgment. They advise me that as I am young, alone, and ill-equipped even to be visiting here, let alone searching for my "friend," that there is nothing better I can do than go home just as soon as the filming is finished, and until then, to stick very close to the crew and my duties. "You have notified the authorities, you have done the best you can," they tell me. I leave the consulate totally dejected and decide that the only thing that feels appropriate to do is to get drunk, though I realize I have gotten this idea from countless different movies, wherein the hero—for it is usually a hero—thus responds to his similarly hopeless-seeming predicament. I blather on about everything to people in the bar, I cry, I realize I am feeling reckless.

The next day a note is left for me at the hotel desk. The note suggests I will soon receive a telephone call that may be of interest to me. At the appointed date and time I do in fact receive a telephone call, in which a man tells me that "some people" don't like what Marina is doing. "Who are these 'some people,'" I ask; "what is Marina doing?" "Some people," is all I am told, as well as that I will receive another call soon. "When," I ask; "Soon," and then a click, is the response. Sitting dumb and chilled in the telephone vestibule, not some five minutes later the desk clerk tells me there is another call on the line for me, this time a woman. She, too, refrains from giving me many details, but suggests I talk to Kitty Dawson, "your rich and famous friend; she can help us. I will call you again, we can meet," the woman says. It occurs to me that I don't really know if the man and the woman are telephoning me together or independently of one another.

That night I dream I go to meet the woman who telephoned me; I arrive at a kind of checkpoint on the edge of the city, and a man with a gun asks me: "Have you come to help us?" And I feel there is a secret password I am supposed to know but don't; the woman on the telephone forgot to give it to me, or she told me and I forgot it.

I don't know what to do next. A movie hero generally has some sort of catharsis following his bar scene, which leads to progress toward his goal. I've certainly never seen any movie with a character facing my current dilemma, but if there were one, it would almost certainly end with tragedy for my character, who would be described as an "idealist" or a "dreamer," my desires to see change in the world would be represented as unrealistic, romantic, youthful, impractical; if I were meant to be a likeable, sympathetic character I would be pretty—even in my rare, and only ever completely understandable, moments of anger. There might be a few saved kittens, smiling old people, perhaps even a bulldozer engine switched off just before the ancient trees fall, but there would be no depictions of significantly tangible results from my character or her comrades' struggles and work. I am an ordinary person, therefore, I cannot effect anything meaningful; if the movie were to be about a great change, or someone who helped bring about great change, say, a Gandhi, then my character early on would be obviously special, noticed by others as such from the start even amidst humble origins.

It's clear a person goes to the movies for some other reason than to see how a story turns out, for in the movies, you always know from the beginning how things will end.

I don't know what I will do, whether I will talk to Kitty, or go meet these people that are telephoning me, or just go home.

"Everyone please stand up! The lion is coming through!" bawls the assistant director. Teddy even stops applying his handkerchief to his dripping forehead, and we all stand at attention; we are to stand because it's best for humans always to be above the height of a lion—if appearing shorter, you present yourself as a thing that can be played with, and play might be wrestling, which the lion enjoys doing while being on top, and you don't want to be under a lion. Though we were told to avoid lengthy direct eye contact as it would be taken as a sign of aggression, our averted gazes still all somehow refer to the honey-colored fur ambling its way onto the set. Conversation only starts up again at the pitch of a reverent whisper. In all the films I've ever made, even a director at the height of respect and authority could not command such a presence, not even Wickwood; not even the most famous actors plying all the tricks of their trade could generate quite such magnetism. The lion, unlike any one of us on set, does not have any of the usual things to lose or win by being here; her motives or possible reactions most of us could not guess at even remotely. We are mesmerized by a creature who we all at once are collectively keenly aware could pose a danger to us, could kill many a type of mammal, even species outweighing our own; but I am at the same time keenly aware this same creature is also being killed in record numbers these days, is rapidly disappearing from this continent, is being hunted and its habitats destroyed. The lioness passes by the assistant director and without missing a step whisks her paw against his ankle. Her trainer chuffs her under the chin, later to explain he was praising her for what was a friendly gesture, though the strength and power of a lion's paw is such that even friendly gestures have been known to knock to the ground a human caught by surprise.

1. Catherine approached me yesterday morning just before shooting began and asked if she could meet with me this evening, seeming not even to have stopped walking up to me before she greeted me and began speaking, seeming to have never stopped walking even as I agreed, and she took her leave of me as quickly and quietly as she had come up to me.

2. When Noel and I spoke on the phone about his plans for us I felt a soothing of something I hadn't before realized needed soothing—it was like something that had never showed its face or form, something lurking in the dark and whose footfalls we only barely sensed, was frightened off when we turned on a porch light.

3. I am so sad when I think of the lions Noel and I saw on safari last year, possibly being hunted by poachers, dying of starvation. I cannot save the lions here on this continent myself, but perhaps Noel and I can give a few lions back home a second chance. It's strange how when

we cannot save something, we are somehow comforted by saving something like it.

Catherine is over three hours late, I don't suppose she is coming after all. I wonder what she could have possibly wanted of me, when she approached me yesterday it surprised me that after all there was something she might have wanted of me. I will never know, I suppose, I doubt I will ever see her again, her work is done here, and the likelihood of our paths crossing again in the future is next to nothing. That is one of the strange things about the motion picture business: you are thrown together with a group of people for a very short time, you work and live together, and sometimes you fall in love with or loathe each other intensely, then as abruptly as it began it is over; the places and the characters disappear as quickly as they came into being, cities and buildings and people suddenly no longer exist; the only proof you have that it all ever existed, that anything happened, is the movie when it finally comes out, and that's nothing you can hold onto; just as soon as you leave the theater, even if you tried to commit them to memory, all the images you saw in the darkness begin to fade and dissolve, you might as well have just dreamed the whole thing. I suppose what is even stranger about the movies is that, whether you are acting in one or watching one, you know very well it's all pretend, but somehow, it still works a sort of spell upon you nonetheless, like those dreams you can't shake when you wake up, and you feel like something, you're not sure what, really did happen.

* Author's note: This quote is based on several variants in circulation ca. 2006, and then often attributed to Lila or Lilla Watson, who is described variously as an "indigenous activist," "Inuit woman," and "Brisbane-based Aboriginal activist and organizer":
    "If you have come to help me (us), you are wasting your time (please go away). But if you have come because (you recognize that) your liberation is bound up with mine (ours), then let us (we can) work (walk) together."

III SOME FILM SCENES FOR WHICH PETER USHER WAS
CINEMATOGRAPHER

1. The sun's glow just beginning to tint the sky, a lioness springs
from a clump of dried grasses and gives chase to a zebra. The
lioness runs and runs, we see her approach first from her left
and then her right and then from behind her; and thus, a distance of eight meters seems to stretch considerably. Again and
again, a massive paw catches the zebra's left hindquarters; the
zebra seems to be slammed to the ground numerous times before the lioness sinks her teeth into the nape of his neck and
grasps his muzzle between her paws, first from one angle, then
another, then another. Still, the sun has hardly moved from
the horizon by the time the lioness begins to drag the zebra
corpse towards a copse of acacia where her pride will come to
share a feast.

*The process from the lioness' charge to the zebra lying motionless
though still alive in the dirt took twenty seconds, though in repre-
sentation it takes five minutes, as each component of the hunt was*

photographed from different angles which are played in sequence, or simply repeated for emphasis. The zebra fell completely limp, though still breathing and not mortally injured, just as soon as the lioness grasped his neck in her teeth; the lioness did not break the skin to accomplish the neckhold, just as she would when grasping her cub in similar fashion. The zebra, upon first contact with the lioness' paw, entered a semiconscious state in which the body's pain and fear are dulled, their signals reduced to something like the sounds of thunderstorms the next valley over; sometimes predators begin a lengthy trek of dragging their prey in such a state not realizing or not caring the animal is not dead, and sometimes the prey is subsequently able to recover and escape in an unguarded moment. The zebra's cause of death was a quick suffocation from his muzzle held tightly closed in the lioness' paws, easily accomplished with the zebra's nervous system immobilizing him. This lioness has only recently begun to hunt alone, when she first began hunting, all the females of her pride would set out to seek prey walking single file or in a loose formation, the first to spot something freezing in place or sinking into cover and all the other lionesses following her example; they would then together stalk closer and closer until a carefully-coordinated attack, in this way, they were able to bring down animals much larger than any of them, such as giraffes. But this lioness' aunts and sisters who taught her to hunt are all dead, and the sisters currently in her pride prefer to hunt alone. Before the meal of the lioness' zebra, for four weeks the camera crew watched the pride feed itself on gazelles killed by several different lone cheetahs, each of whom was still exhausted from the hunt and easy to scare off. The oldest lion was observed happily feeding from a half-eaten antelope carcass of unknown provenance. The camera crew knew the hours of the day when the lions were likeliest to be active, but still the majority of the lions' time was spent sleeping or resting, with frequent gestures of affection towards one another such as head rubbing, licking, and general touching. "What do you mean the lions haven't attacked anything yet?" crackled the producer over the line late one night, regular office hours for him.

"Kill, attack, that's what lions do, everybody knows that! King of the jungle and all that! That's what people will pay to see! That's what I'm paying you to get!" As the lioness with the zebra awaited the arrival of her pride in the shelter of the thorny acacias, she again clasped her paws around the zebra's head but only to gently hold it steady as she licked the zebra's forehead and ears, much as she has groomed her own cubs. *"I don't see any point in including that,"* the producer declared, *"kind of anticlimactic... confusing, really."*

2. A lion cub walks across a plain dotted with dried grasses towards a tree where earlier, adjacent to the tree trunk, a man clad in khaki, a rifle strapped over his shoulder, broad-brimmed hat ineffectively shading his pink face from the intense light of the sun, stealthily concealed a metal trap with dry grass. Arriving at the tree close to where the trap is concealed, the lion cub sniffs around, seeming puzzled, and looks warily into branches overhead. Another cub's cry is heard from the right, and the lion jerks his head towards the cry and then begins to walk in the direction of it, but when another cub's cry is heard from the left, he stops and looks back and forth a few times before a look of understanding and determination crosses his face, he changes direction, and proceeds to the left.

Five times before, the cub was called to the tree to find a cube of fresh meat lay on the spot where the trap was then subsequently placed at the same time that the tree was doused with a mix of pungent aftershaves. At the cub's sixth approach to the tree, two people crept up to short distances from either side of the tree while the cub was occupied with studying the fresh scents of the aftershave and checking to confirm no more chunks of meat had been placed in the vicinity; as soon as the cub exhibited less than total interest in what his nose was telling him, first one, then the other person, shook a metal dish in the fashion they had been doing prior to offering the cub his daily ration over the preceding couple of weeks. The shaking alternated several times, *and then the person on the right revealed his metal dish to be completely empty, and then the person on the left revealed his dish contained some meat and bones, which he then lowered to the ground.*

3. A glass-sided tank of indeterminate dimensions is framed with a horizon line such that the realms of underwater and above water are equally visible. "Here comes the Professor!" says the voiceover, as above the water a smiling blonde man wearing horn-rimmed glasses and yellow rubber waterproof outerwear appears with a bucket just as a dolphin appears under the water. The man slaps a dead mullet on the surface of the water mimicking a live mullet's tail motions before tossing it aloft and the dolphin arcs upward in a splash to fetch it. "And Billy earns his first fish of the day!" Another dolphin, then another, then another enter the frame, each to receive his own appetizer. "And here's Dippy, Dandy, and Scotty!" The four begin to cavort together: here two pairs, there three and one, then a knot of four; slithering along and around one anothers' sleek gray forms, every couple of moments a pair of heads so close as to appear to be atop the same body erupting above the surface of the water in crests of choppy waves, every couple of moments one or two dolphins disentangling from the frenetic knitting of fins and flippers so as to redouble efforts to crash back into one another. One of the dolphins breaks away from the group repeatedly in order to linger against the frothing jet of the water intake, swaying and rocking gently as he does so.

The dolphins' erect penises are not visible in any of the frames.

"They're a mighty playful bunch, aren't they? But here's something that will turn them serious." A sand-bar shark, a turtle and some small fish approach, and the braid of four dolphins begins to writhe in unison in the general direction of the sand-bar shark. After a moment, they dissolve their group embrace and each take turns projecting themselves towards the shark, sometimes with such force he is pushed to the side of the tank, and after awhile longer, in twos and three and again a knot of four, they descend upon the sand-bar shark with great vigor. The frame is now viewed through a different panel of the tank.

One of the dolphin's attempts to insert his penis in the soft tissues at the rear of the turtle's shell would be prominently visible from the first camera position.

From this new panel, the lone dolphin and turtle pair is mostly eclipsed by the other three dolphins alternating in butting the sand-bar shark. "Though the dolphin is a cheerful fellow, he is not afraid to act defensively against an adversary whose presence he resents or considers dangerous."

4. Three grizzly bears splash about in rushing, rocky rapids, in time with a whimsical tune that conjures old-time American folk dances with a twangy banjo and jaunty fiddle taking precedence over the background synthesizers. Again and again the bears dive and roll underwater, occasionally displacing smaller rocks with the motions of their massive paws. The frame shifts upward to record the stands of fir trees and mountains in the distance as the music merges into swelling horns and strings conveying the transcendence of big-sky country expansiveness, and a confident male voiceover intones, "This is nature as it is... a landscape of authenticity, purity... These bears play in pristine bathwater, their view free from any of the trappings of civilization."

The bears, had they not been moving quickly or obscured by water and rocks, would have been seen to be severely underweight, their pelts hanging loosely from their bones. Not normally given to lengthy play in the water, they were desperately seeking fish carcasses they may have somehow missed in their fishing, as the salmon run for the third year in a row was such that less than a quarter of the usual number of fish swam upstream into the bears' territory; scientists studying the salmon were not sure whether changes in ocean conditions or hydroelectric plants sited along the river had more impact upon the salmon no longer spawning as usual. The Kennetusic nation, who has fished for salmon in the Kennetasawak river alongside their sister and brother bears ever since the Creator ate the seeds of the lodgepole pine and spat up First Man and First Woman, have called a council of elders; many people have had dreams of ill portents relating to the salmon.

5. A pair of Damson's Winterducks builds a nest in the rocks at the edge of the water. One of the ducks goes in search of food and brings back a small mouthful for the other duck who has remained in the nest cuddling her eggs. "Isn't he a dutiful husband?" asks a debonair male voiceover.

Both ducks are female; the Damson's Winterduck does not exhibit sexual dimorphism in its markings, and definitive gender identification by a human is accomplished at closer range than is photography. Female Winterducks do not always parent with the same duck that fertilized their eggs, and frequently choose female partners; male Winterducks also pair up and sometimes take over an abandoned nest containing eggs, or build a nest together.

The eggs hatch and the duck parents take turns seeking food for the five ducklings; one of the ducklings is much smaller than the others; his brothers and sisters grow a bit faster and consequently become better able to jostle themselves into more prominent positions each time a duck parent returns with food.

The duck parents exhaust themselves flying back and forth to the nest; they are mobbed each time they arrive, and in the frenzy they cannot ever count how many mouths they've just filled.

Eventually the small duckling dies. The duck parents try to gather him underneath their wings and place food in his bill but his limp neck flops, and then they pause and look at him. The voiceover concludes, "At first it may not seem fair, but in nature, some must die so that others may live. Everything Nature has designed has a purpose, even violence and death. In this way, she keeps her world in balance, and makes it a place of overarching order and beauty."

6. A haphazard group of lions and one tiger lounge in and around the dilapidated ruins of a house situated next to a stream in the bottom of a valley. Kitty Dawson and a man clad in khaki, a rifle strapped over his shoulder, broad-brimmed hat ineffectively shading his pink face from the intense light of the sun, pull up near the cats in a Land Rover and photograph the scene. One of the lions approaches the Rover and sniffs it, pulling himself up onto his hindlegs and placing his paws on the trunk. Suddenly, it is night in roughly the same spot, and masked individuals approach with torches and alight the ruins of the house; a lone lion approaches and roars. Kitty Dawson appears suddenly, carrying a cub out of the burning ruins.

After eight weeks of shooting the camera crew cannot afford to work further without receiving pay, and no further footage is shot.

7. "Vicious, inexplicable attack at wild animal park caught on film!" declares a strident male voiceover as an elephant stampedes into a group of flimsy huts, flailing his trunk and ears. "One employee was injured, and scores of visitors had the fright of their lives at Chacamac Lake Safari Animal Park today when a rampaging elephant breached three layers of high-tech

enclosures and demolished some decorative structures before heading for a concession area. Professional wildlife cinematographer Peter Usher happened to be visiting the park with his family and caught it all on tape. Local sheriff's deputies raced to the scene and, finding the elephant pinning a park employee against a concession stand with his foot and appearing to prepare to gore him with his tusks, shot the animal. The employee was released from Presbyterian United Hospital later this afternoon. A spokesperson for Chacamac Lake Safari Park said the elephant had never exhibited any unusual behavior before, and explained that experts currently believe that sudden violent behavior in elephants such as this is rare but documented, and is likely caused by hormonal surges."

Nine years earlier, one afternoon while the elephant alternately nibbled at tender leaves and suckled his mother, who fed alongside his aunts and older sister in the lush, shaded understory of the forest, the family was ambushed by hunters; the elephant watched his mother, aunts, and sister fall to the ground bleeding. That he was so young and had only milk tusk precursors saved his life at the time, and he was quickly tethered with intricate knots to both of the hunters' jeeps before the hunters set about wrenching and sawing the tusks out of his family's heads, starting with his sister, while she still waved her legs about weakly. In the pads of his feet the elephant could feel some of his kind moving some distance away; he wished he could tell them what was happening, but did not know how. The elephant was dragged along behind the hunters' vehicles a great distance before being transferred into the custody of other men who drove him into an enclosure by hitting him with metal chains, then other men came and quarreled loudly with the men who'd received him from the men who killed his family; the sum to be exchanged between the two groups was quite large, many times the annual income for the average citizen scraping by through farming, but both parties worried they were risking too much for too little a profit; each group contained men who wanted to feed their families well and send them places they heard were safer and better, as well as single men who wanted prestige, luxuries, pleasures and comfort. Some of the men did not enjoy the actions they were taking, while others were not fazed by them or even took pleasure in some aspects of them, and all of the men tried very hard not to think about the serious and violent things that might befall them as a result of the actions they were taking. After they all calmed down, the new men chased the elephant into a truck and drove him to the coast where he was loaded into a large ship that took him across an ocean, and when the ship made landfall, he was loaded into another truck that drove a very long time before it arrived at the Chacamac Lake Safari Animal Park, where he was placed in an open-air grassy enclosure, from the edges of which people stood all day and watched him. On soft dirt for the first time in weeks, he placed his trunk to the ground but neither it nor his four feet could detect the vibrations of any others of his kind within a few days' walk. He listened for hours at a time for days on end, the only thing ever sounding remotely like some of his kind being the occasional echoes of thunderstorms some miles away. After some time, he gave up his listening.

" I hope the next time my wife has a hormonal surge she doesn't breach any enclosures!" says the man newscaster. " I've been to Chacamac Lake with my family," coos the woman newscaster, "it's very naturalistic, with big spaces for the animals, just like they'd have in the wild." "Yes," says the man newscaster, "the habitats there are much bigger than regular zoo cages... guess that elephant didn't realize how good he actually had it."

8. A spotlight cuts jagged swathes through the darkness, reflecting glare on steel bars of cages and illuminating the pale faces of the baby chimps within them. The chimps' eyes have been sewn shut with thick black sutures. The chimps do not move even as their cages are opened. "The designers of this experiment conduct it in order to test their hypothesis that

infants deprived of sensory stimulation, including contact with a mother, will not mature in the same fashion as those that are not so deprived," a male narrator tells us. "If this hypothesis were to be amply proven to be fact, and this experiment and others related to it—such as kittens whose heads and paws are encased in purpose-built plastic boxes—were deemed no longer necessary, then the designers would no longer receive grant money to cover their salaries and those of their assistants, the lab would be closed and given over to other researchers who would refit it for another experiment, and Hudson's Biological Supplies would have to find another customer to purchase baby monkeys at $3,000 apiece." The film quality changes and six longtailed monkeys wearing tiny metal helmets are being held in the arms of humans wearing black ski masks. A seventh monkey is being attended to on a tabletop by two more humans also wearing black ski masks. The voiceover explains, "These monkeys were just rescued from an experiment in which their heads were cemented into helmets attached to wires attached to a pneumatic device that slammed the monkeys' heads at a sixty-degree angle at a force of up to 1,000 g's or, 1,000 times the force of gravity. It has been long known that a force of only 15 g's can kill a human being." Suddenly the screen appears blurred, its edges unevenly framed by the folds of the lab coat in which the camera is concealed. Piglets are strapped into elaborate restraints; each has a large opening in its abdomen where the skin has been removed, and to which various substances are applied, and a tiny intravenous drip is connected to each piglet's left foreleg. Excrement and urine fill the bottoms of their cages. A laboratory worker accompanying the one secretly filming the piglets laughs and jokes as they go about their duties. "This little asshole tried to bite me yesterday," the worker says of one of the piglets, and thrusts the feeding syringe into the piglet's mouth with such force she gags and chokes, spattering the gruel-like substance down her chin and onto the floor of her cage.

Though pigs' livers function in many ways very differently than those of humans, the drug company sponsoring the experiment will get the drug being tested on the piglets approved for use in humans after it is demonstrated that the drug does not cause cancer of the liver in a statistically meaningful percentage of the piglets. Of all the drugs and substances tested in the lab on various animals and approved for use in humans, approximately fifty-four percent of them—consistent with the same ratio of all drugs and substances tested in labs across the country in the latter part of the twentieth century—after a number of years of use in the general population, will eventually be found to cause adverse reactions in humans leading to injury or even death that were not foreshadowed in the reactions the animals had to the drugs and substances.

A
N
I
M
A
L

56

S
A
N
C
T
U
A
R
Y

IV   NATURE FILMS

Mr. Wickwood, Man's Best Friend was a commercial success despite the critics—at the time—disparaging it. Now, twelve years later, however, it is receiving more positive critical reconsideration. Though at the time of its release it was deemed shocking and lacking in artfulness, now some feel it presaged the stylistic innovations of your most recent films, and a number of younger directors, particularly avant-garde Europeans such as Quinn Markman and Thierry Franchot, cite its influence on their own aesthetics. Can you discuss how you came to make it, what you thought of it at the time, how you think of it now?

Oh yes, the reviews on that one were something: of course what was a "disappointment" and a "rather cheap and sensationalist effort" was not only a commercial success itself but ushered in an era of money-making imitations even more offensive in brutality and vulgarity, none of which ever received as much critical wrath as the source of all that they ripped-off. The idea for this film was brought about through an utterly illogical process, a sort of a happy accident. For her twelfth birthday my daughter received a docile silky-blonde cocker spaniel, Guinevere, and we were obliged—largely at the urging of all our neighbors, who assured us that it was simply how it was done—to hire a professional trainer to come to the house and instruct both girl and dog in playing their appropriate roles. In our rather middling middle-class house, which the studio had found for us when we first moved to the States, my library looked out over the lawn on which the dog-and-daughter lessons took place twice a week. One afternoon I was distracted overhearing poor Guinevere repeatedly entreated to fetch, fetch, fetch; this troubled me greatly, and I could not think why, until I imagined I heard my granny's voice saying "fetch," and then I remembered her using this word somehow in a way I had never understood as a child. It had been clearly curious and ominous, I was certain it had conveyed something sinister, I began to suspect it was a meaning particular to her native Connemara, and I could not get the damned word out of my head, and so I consulted the *Oxford English Dictionary's* fertile repository of meanings antique, obsolete, and esoteric. And sure enough, "fetch" can metamorphose from a doing into a being, it can be a noun meaning an apparition, the double of a living being who comes to bring a message to the original that it mirrors. This double can bring tidings of either a happy longevity or immediate dissolution. Well, this was no surprise coming from my granny—many of the supernatural figures and customs she whispered about to me when I was a boy possessed contradictory, dualist natures: a fairy met upon the road might just as easily help as hinder you, a dream of a wedding could portend either a birth or a death. It was my granny who taught me well that we are citizens of a realm where at best we only ever have a fifty-fifty chance.

"Fetch, fetch, fetch," forever echoing from across the lawn, I was immediately occupied with envisioning how a dog's "fetch" might just as easily be man's worst enemy as he is man's best friend. Man's best friend, indeed—how can a creature that is first and foremost obedient ever be a trusted friend? It fears you, and does what you want so long as it remains scared, unless it should come to fear your adversary more—at which point, it changes sides and turns on you.

I set about writing the screenplay. The plot of *Man's Best Friend* is absurd on paper, but of course many films succeed precisely because the plot eventually steps aside and lets other things be accomplished. In the case of this film, the fact that aside from lengthy protracted

scenes of chaos, not a whole lot actually happens—and the underlying reasons behind what
does happen are never bothered about—the
dearth of plot eventually permits the viewer to
focus on other details, and it was those details
I slavishly recreated from my observations;
everything from a patrolman's swagger to an
average schoolchild's box lunch to the tex-
ture and rhythm of the rows of shrubbery-em-
braced driveways that suburban-dwellers feel
they must impose upon the landscape.

I really wanted the American viewer first to
see a world so very like his own, perhaps even
slightly improved, so that he might wish he
could step into the screen and inhabit it, and
then just as soon as he did, he would realize
he was actually trapped in a place where his
most fundamental assumptions and cherished
ways of life would quickly become impossible:
what he had always thought of as completely
under his control, dutifully affectionate, and
in service to him, suddenly and without warning would defy all attempts at submission and
comprehension, and turn murderous and un-
predictable.

Fetch, fetch, fetch. I wanted to call the film
Fetch, but they wouldn't let me, those people
to whom I always plead my case, who approve
how much I get to spend on the ladies' dresses,
who I usually can coax into permitting me quite
a lot they don't seem to really understand but
who on occasion must make a show of know-

ing better than I about certain things. When I explained the double-entendre of "fetch" and how it had inspired the entire concept for the screenplay, I was met with blank stares. The sharpest of the bunch added, after a brief silence, that such allusions would be utterly lost on American audiences. I tried to explain that what I really wanted was to subtly convey that the out-of-control dogs were fetches, doubles in a sense, not just for gentle pets, but also for humans. That a middle-class person is so very like a well-trained dog himself, so dutifully coming and going between home and work, at work a top dog barking down his orders, at home the endless duties to fulfill in exchange for small treats and a warm bed; and were he not carefully schooled in so many laws and customs and procedures to obey, in respect of the watchdogs of morality, society, and etiquette, he would revert to a less-obedient animality he pretends not to have in common with other mammals, including untrained dogs. I wanted to show each successful executive, every popular ladies' auxiliary president, that they were at their present "top dog" position in the food chain not by the law of some god or hypothesized organizing force of nature, but through habitual conditioning, a great deal of chance, and some measure of stratagem that might at any time fail; I wanted to show that a coup d'etat was possible at any time. Though my budget-minders were hardly warming to me after this speech, having had a very fine brandy after our lunch I was emboldened to press my philosophical musings even further: "I'm going to imply an ambiguity as to whether certain acts of violence were committed by dog or man, showing how tenuous "natural order" is, blurring the boundaries between the species—that sort of thing!" I blubbered out, if memory serves me correctly. At this, the smartest of the studio executives nervously said: "You mean... you want to make a werewolf picture!?"

My stupefaction was mistaken for a submissive pose, and so he quickly continued: "Why, that's about ten years out of fashion, Mr. Wickwood! We've come to count on you for breaking new ground, creating new trends!"

Now, I don't really ever enjoy discussing beforehand with anybody else just how it is I intend to pull off one of my stories. It always seems to come down to trying to describe in words how I am going to show something visual by not-showing it: a perverse impossible task of the type gods or devils set before an unlucky soul. Of course now with all you university people taking movies so seriously, there's plenty of books that explain all my methods and theories quite succinctly, making it all look like it was rather easy, but back then, at that moment I felt completely unequipped to parse a few words to assure some very literal-minded pencil-pushers that my explorations of rather murky territory would come to visual and narrative fruition, and be wholly unrelated to the previously-known cinematic world's treatment of species ambiguity wherein some hammy actor might declaim with dyed wool affixed to his face with spirit gum. So I retreated: Yes, of course, the film would be simply "nature" run amok, with humans eventually finding some respite in the end.

"We like the title your wife suggested," they said. "*Man's Best Friend*? We're permitting you then at least a little irony in your title after all, are we not, Mr. Wickwood?" In the end, the studio was quite happy. This was the third picture into my contract to deliver six total to make audiences anxious, frightened, and feeling a bit clever at the end; and it was ahead of schedule and close to budget—and dogs were considerably cheaper to hire than human actors, not a union member among them.

I think the American studio, given recent events relating to missiles and a certain Caribbean nation, might have preferred a film where the message was more stridently: "Four legs bad, two legs good!" I myself am personally of the camp of "Four legs—who can really say? Two legs—quite likely bad, often even in spite of decent intentions."

Kitty, last week you mentioned that you were reminded of a recurring dream you had while you were pregnant. We got off on another tangent, which I think was very fruitful, but today I'd like to pick up there if that's alright with you—would you like to tell me about this dream?

Yes, yes of course, if you think it's important. I... I haven't had the dream since I gave birth to Rory. I don't remember why I brought it up last week, do you...?

I'll remind you in a moment but first, while you're fresh, why don't you just tell me the dream?

OK, well, in the dream, it's as if I wasn't actually asleep, or perhaps I'm asleep within the dream... I get up, and I leave the house while everyone is sleeping, I leave without waking anyone, and I begin to walk at a lumbering pace, struggling to propel my big pregnant belly forward, and as I walk down the street and past the houses my belly begins to shrink a bit. I feel lighter, and I pick up the pace, which seems to make my belly shrink faster, and this gives me greater strength, as if I am absorbing some kind of sustenance, like a camel draws nourishment from its stored-up hump, and I realize it is a glorious cycle, and I want to hasten its progression, and soon I am running out of the town, into the country, towards the woods, and the moon is full above me, and I am slim and lithe and quick. I feel no sense of loss at the transformation of the baby because there was no death, I... I feel I still carry the same life-force within me, only rather than a weight or density it has been transmuted, it is now fluid and hot and running all through my veins. Free of the bulge at my waist I can lunge forward in a more... efficient posture, and before I know it my hands drop to the ground and assume a gallop as steadily as my feet. I can feel the dew falling, sweet and heavy against my skin, and the gravitational force of the moon seems to exert... a tidal pull, on the fluids in the air and in the viscera of my flesh, it pulls me farther and farther away from my family, from people altogether, further towards the woods, and when I pass into the dark cover of trees and bramble, I realize my skin is not scratched and torn by the thorns and twigs of the underbrush because I have a thick coat of fur, the thickets comb my pelt, and my hide shivers with plea-sure at this... and I feel more and more alive in direct proportion to how far into the forest I run. I find myself twitching my nose and flar-ing my big nostrils... uh, all the better to smell with, my dear... (giggles nervously)

(neutral pause) Yes, go on...

... and, the simplest scents give me cause to pause and discern every layered note within a single whiff. It's like I'm winnowing through the molecules of odor ferried on the wind, I can ascertain the portraits and signatures of wet maple leaves, moss, rabbit dung, fir nee-dles, the warm feathers of a roosting owl from one puff of a breeze... and to do this seems the highest art-form, an activity that uses all my... sensory and analytic powers all at once, and to their fullest expressions, and I am more... sat-isfied than I can ever remember having been.

Some nights I discern a repeating pattern of scents, which turns into a path that I follow. Some nights I follow a path until I catch sight of something or someone else, usually a small creature oblivious to my approach; and at this, my mouth begins to water, and I move forward possessed by a... a kind of a lust, so consuming that it effaces from memory all the sensations and actions that follow... so the dream goes on but I don't actually remember the end, I only remember it up to this point.

And you had this dream while you were pregnant, but you haven't had it since you've given birth?

Yes, yes. Now, last week when I brought this dream up, I...

Well Kitty, before I say anything else, I'd like to hear what you think it all means.

Well, this sounds strange, but... to me it doesn't feel like it means anything. I feel like the dream's purpose was not to mean something, but just to be... like, an actual experience, I mean, I felt so alive in this dream, more alive than when I'm awake!

Uh-huh... do you have any ideas about what the animal could symbolize? What kind of animal is it, exactly?

Well, it's not a symbolic animal to me, it's a very specific animal, it's not an animal of a type of species that I know exists, it's a creature that I and the baby turn into, it's still us.

I see...Well, the disappearance of the baby and the pregnancy is quite notable, don't you think? Do you think the dream could have reflected fears you may have about your changing body during pregnancy?

Well... no... I mean, for one thing, Noel found me very attractive throughout my pregnancy, "my little fertility goddess," he called me... we actually, well, I began to feel more pleasure when we... we felt closer than we ever had before...

Uh-huh, well, some women do report increased libido with all the hormonal changes of pregnancy. Changes in hormones can influence all sorts of changes in behavior. But in your dream, the baby disappears as you feel more... uh, do you think you had subconscious doubts, that once the baby comes you wouldn't feel as, uh, close to your husband? On some subconscious level, is it possible you worried the baby would come between you? Could you be feeling that Rory, now, a couple years old, is the source of some of your problems with your husband?

Well... no! ... and, and, it's not that I necessarily feel more attractive as the animal, I feel... more alive... and, like I said, it doesn't feel like the baby disappears... it's like I am a woman with a baby inside me, and then together we shift into something else, that has different... I don't know... abilities? powers?

So you see the baby as power? Or as a person, completely in your power, a subset of you... do you think this is related to your persistent fantasies of breast-feeding?

Well, I don't think that's why I wanted to breast-feed Rory, to have power over him! I just love him so much, and... when I look at the cats at the sanctuary, when I look at other animals nursing their young, they are so loving and protective... I wish I could have done the same for my own baby, I think about how I could have eaten the best and purest foods, and then these would have been broken down and used in my body to make milk just for my baby, my very own milk, I just wish I could have given him such a pure and rare substance... I suppose it's also amazing that it's even possible I could have given him something that's... well, made out of my very own flesh! How intense, it's like... I don't know, you know, like in the Catholic mass, with the bread and the wine being body and blood, I imagine... I mean, I'm not religious now, but the idea of how like Jesus, acting out of love, and loving so much, he just wanted to give of himself the most he could possibly give... and then there is this connection, this intense connection of love...

Perhaps next time we can discuss your early religious training. But for now... Kitty, I think it's important you see you've done your best and done what's best for your son. After all, it's 1972, we're

A
N
I
M
A
L

68

S
A
N
C
T
U
A
R
Y

well into the 20ᵗʰ century, and we've seen enormous progress in science and medicine... Leading medical experts have concluded that we have improved on breast-feeding with the modern, scientific formulas. I know in the last few years some people have been advocating a return to breastfeeding, these types of people coming out of the hippie movement, who claim without any clinical evidence whatsoever to back them up, that whatever's "natural" is always best in any given situation, but there is no proof, no study showing breastfeeding is better, and plenty showing how effective these modern formulas are. What could be more hygienic and nutritious than something modern scientists have worked out carefully in a laboratory, that is produced under stringent, consistent conditions in a state-of-the-art factory?

Well, when you put it like that... but, so many species... for thousands of, millions of, I guess, years, so much life has been supported by... I don't understand how... it just feels so, well, I mean, for a mother to be able to...

Kitty, I'm afraid our time is almost up for this week, and I'd like to just ask you one more time what you think this dream could mean, what you think the animal could symbolize.

Well, I really... I think this dream felt to me... I don't know, more... special, or... sacred, or something than just some sort of secret coded guide to some part of my consciousness that evidently hides from me. I feel like we can't ever guess at its full importance by killing it and putting it on the dissection table... like, if you took one of the beautiful, fascinating cats from the sanctuary and just shot him and cut him open and looked at his dead organs and his limbs that no longer move, we would see certain things, but would that really be any more helpful to anybody to learn what that cat is like than it would be to just live with him, and watch and interact with him, and...?

Alright Kitty, I'm sorry, our time is up and we're really going to have to stop now. Have a good weekend, and see you next week.

Mr. Wickwood, can you discuss your methods of working with actors? You are legendary for eliciting amazing performances from actors who never again in their careers managed to top the work they did for you, though there have been occasional protests that you can be unsettling, that you've gone too far in certain ways.

Oh it's the cliché, isn't it, but one well-founded in truth: how is any creative person, an artist of any sort, not a bit unbalanced, not a bit willing to go farther than someone else might? Even just to think straight and do your work, you have to repeatedly shut yourself up alone in some room somewhere, ignoring those who might care about you or need you... Just to finish something properly, even a modest painting or book, requires such focus and persistence, the marshaling of resources usually beyond your own fiscal capacity, and usually against so many people saying "no" to you for various, usually quite logical reasons: those who care about you wonder whether you shouldn't be working at something useful, how you'll pay the rent; those that don't know you from Adam, well, what's this bit of rot, then, that you expect them to put up on their gallery wall or publish, who is it that you said you knew...?

How many stories have we in which a person struggles for years with most everyone telling him he's a bunch of shite, eventually dying penniless and friendless in an attic, but down the road his paintings end up hung on the walls of museums, or his books taught in university courses? In any other situation in life, if you kept at something with the same odds of success and against the same degree of protestations, you'd do well to have your head examined, certainly, if you pursued a woman with the same disregard for rejection, you could be put in jail. But that's precisely how you have to pursue your art in order to realize it.

So, just to make anything, really, is a sort of pathological miracle, but when your medium is filmmaking, you really have to become earnest about your pathology, because it's not just you sitting in your little room painting or writing, no, you have a whole lot of people standing around waiting for you, you have a full crew and all the actors and all the equipment and maybe the weather all wanting to behave however they like, and you have to get it all to work together, on time, to make your picture.

My methods... there's an element of directing that is not unlike what I've read is the task of a general engaged in guerrilla warfare: plan, plan, plan, but at the same time always be improvising according to how the wind is blowing, what resources are unexpectedly made available to you or taken from you. Actors are the most unstable elements a director deals with... I can't say I have some overriding philosophy about how to get them to do their work, except that obviously, these actors who are nowadays so concerned about their characters' "motivations," well, they certainly have their own differing motivations for doing what it is you want them to, some of them want to please you, some of them want to compete with you, some of them need to prove their father wrong, some of them need to look prettier than anyone else around... and so there are all these different sorts of dances you do in response to each actor's sensibilities... I'm a big fan of nature films, you know, little documentaries showing things like the Red-crested Shermot's intricate method of swinging his elaborate tailfeathers around to attract his mate, and how she either accepts his gift of an insect or walks away disdainfully after soiling it with the dust from her claws, Mr. Shermot looking so serious the whole time he wiggles his coronet-like backside; then in the next week's program, we're treated to perhaps the brutish head-buttings of bighorn rams, who'd trip over their own hooves if they tried to do a single step of Mr. Shermot's mating cha-cha, but if on the other hand they decided to take on the bonnet of your car, you'd be in for some serious repairs. There's a constant interplay of lyricism and force I find stimulating, nature films, I never tire of them, each species so different and going about getting what it needs with feathers, fins, and whiskers specially suited to the task through centuries of genetic refinement, always in the end, no matter how graceful, baroque, or exotic the feathers or fins or whiskers may be, the story always boils down to the tale of a creature engaged in a struggle of life or death. At the same time, these films often give me a laugh, as I imagine actors I've worked with going through their own individual elaborate rituals, looking as simultaneously beautiful and ridiculous as the rarest jungle bird, and all the while taking the whole thing so very seriously, while we look on.

Good heavens, with some actors it's been a good thing I'd watched so many nature films. Cory Johnson, if we couldn't keep him away from the bottle, it was like having a wounded bear loose on the set. And in *Man's Best Friend*, Kitty Dawson responded best to some of the methods the trainers used with their dogs, you know: we want you to move towards this direction, so here's a little something tasty for you to come and get; okay, now we want you to move away from this direction, so we're going to shine bright lights and make scary noises at you.

Kitty, I'd like to talk about how you came to start this... animal sanctuary that you've got going. Can you tell me, first, what your motivations were, for starting it?

My motivations... well, I had no premeditated plan to do this! I mean, I've always really loved animals, but I certainly never set out thinking I'd have a bunch of lions and tigers to care for... it just kind of happened!

So... you feel like it happened beyond your control?

Oh, no, no, no! I just mean, the way it happened, it happened so fast, sometimes it seems a bit... well, we put the thing into motion when Noel and I decided to assemble a small cast, as it were, for the movie we wanted to make, so we put out the word that we might want to borrow a few lions for awhile, and rented a piece of property out in the hills... we'd scarcely put up the fencing when people started telling us about abandoned and neglected big cats they'd heard about, stories to break your heart, and in some cases, people started anonymously dropping cats off in the middle of the night. Someone just locked Simba and Sasha's collars to the fence one night, when they were cubs...

Kitty, why do you think it's your responsibility to care for all of these animals? Don't you think someone with more experience, specialized knowledge, say, would be a more logical choice? Aren't there already places established where these animals could go, places run by people who have training, and better suited to this sort of thing? Wouldn't it be better off leaving this kind of thing to experts?

Well, I don't think it's more my responsibility to care for these animals than it is anybody else's, if that's what you mean, I think it's all our responsibility, except, well, nobody else seemed to be being responsible when it came to some of these animals, and there they were, in front of me... really, it's that simple: we met these animals, they needed help, nobody else really wanted to deal with it, and we had the choice either to ignore them or help them somehow ourselves... I mean, of course, people have helped *us* enormously, once we put it out there, what we were doing... and no, I mean, there are other animal sanctuaries in the country, but they already have more animals than they know what to do with, they don't have infinite room, and we did try to find places for these animals, but they would be, well, killed, if there wasn't anyplace else for them to go. We do of course consult with people who have a lot of experience in these matters, they've just already got a lot to deal with so they can't take primary responsibility for these animals, but they give us advice and also point us towards how we can educate ourselves...

This is all also enormously expensive to maintain, how do you intend to pay for it all, over time? Have you thought that far ahead?

Yes, yes, we're in the process of applying for it to be non-profit, like a charity, so we can receive donations that people can write off their taxes.

Well it seems like an awful lot of work. Do you feel you will be able to balance your responsibilities to the animals with those to your husband and son, and an acting career?

Well, Noel's involved just as much as I am and... hopefully Rory will find it interesting to grow up around all these animals...

What is it about the animals themselves that interests you?

Well... they're just such fascinating and beautiful creatures, when I've been to Africa and seen them in the wild, I just thought they were astonishing, and these animals in particular are so far from where they belong, some of them have suffered so much... getting to know them as individuals, well now, they're my friends and family.

Kitty, what do you think of the idea that some peo-

ple focus their emotions on animals because they're safer to relate to than other humans...

This is the first time someone's suggested that these big 400-pound cats with their teeth and claws are safer than my toddler and husband! Even if you met my mother-in-law, I think...

Well, by "safer" we mean, because animals can't talk back to us, they're like blank screens upon which we can just project what we want them to seem like they're feeling, we can pretend that they are loving us, understanding us... we anthropomorphize them, we make them in our image. Do you think it's possible you are projecting anything onto the animals?

Well, I don't know about the fact they can't talk back... I mean, not in English, but they certainly do seem to communicate effectively enough in their own ways... I mean, I see what you're saying, but I think some of them do love and understand us and each other, I don't think that's all pretend, and if you learn about animals, you start to read their actions correctly, not just on human terms... I don't really know how you can generalize about all animals, either... anyway... it's kind of funny, when you say animals are like blank screens, this reminds me, some directors I've worked with, when I was meant to express an emotion onscreen, in a moment where I was meant to be still and not talking, rather than try to summon up what the emotion was meant to be, they told me just to look straight ahead and think of nothing at all at during those moments, that the audience would project what it wanted to see on me, or, as Wickwood put it, the audience would see in the look in my eyes what he'd spent the entire movie up until that scene carefully orchestrating them to want to see in the look in my eyes. I always thought this was interesting, how this worked, because it did work... I mean, some people obviously just project what they want to on other people, let alone animals, and some people just won't acknowledge anything in a person or an animal except what they want to. Wickwood, I don't know what it was he saw, if it was there or if he made it, when we were filming, sometimes it reminded me of when my father and my brother would go hunting... then, there was much waiting and watching of movement, slow, slow, slow, and then all of the sudden, when they decided it was the right time, all of a sudden—pow! And with Wickwood, each take, he would set us up by giving us some cryptic directions, he would get mad if we tried to get him to explain any further, and really mad if we ever said how we thought we might feel or what we might do if we were the character in the situation ourselves, and so then, when it came to filming, it seemed like he would sort of start the action, turn us loose a bit confused, and then let us go and go and go, and he would wait and wait and wait until he saw what it was he was looking for, and then suddenly there was—"Cut!" And it felt like, sometimes, that word felt so literal, like some sort of violence, sometimes I would be doing a scene, and I would be so confused or frightened, not really understanding what Wickwood wanted from me, just kind of trying to move through space, the world would begin to blur around me as I would do a scene like this, and then I would hear "Cut!" and it was almost like the crack of a hunter's gun, it would take place often at some point when I wasn't expecting it, almost as if it were at the moment I let down my guard, or something, and of course, working with him, I began to look forward to that moment of "Cut," it began to feel like such relief, even though at the same time, it was frightening... always, everything ended with "Cut," everything depended on ending, everything ended when he said it did, the last word, the director always has the last word, when you are making a movie, your whole life rests each day when the director says it does... it's funny how they say, don't they, that things are captured by film, captured on film... sometimes to me, it felt like we were turned loose to run free for a few minutes until we were captured, over and over and over again, like some awful hunting game... and what was it that was being captured, exactly, it was like something was being taken from us at some crucial moment, they call them takes, after all, don't they, it was like...

Kitty, I'm sorry, we are out of time, we have to stop for now.

Mr. Wickwood, let's turn to your most recent film now, Interrogation. *You are at the height of your career, with access to a large budget and many re-sources. You could afford to make a film in exotic, far-flung locations with a league of high-paid actors, and yet you now choose to give us, for the most part of the film, two people in a stark, drab room that could be anywhere. Of course you have the formidable and in-demand Robert Sunderland, but you have as the female lead cast young newcomer Emily Marshall. And if that's not risky enough, you never reveal who the interrogator is, exactly: is he a policeman or officer of the law, some sort of person involved with a criminal organization, or just a lone psychopath?*

Well, you should choose whichever of those scares you the most! You can project any of those things onto the character, or perhaps a combination...

Well, that's precisely where there has been some controversy... Can you discuss just what it is you had in mind when you made this film?

The short answer to that question would be: Emil Meyer. You know, that's where I really first learned the movie business, Germany, 1926, watching Emil Meyer make *Die Befragungen,* "*The Interrogations.*" I'd been working my way up in London in Tellington Studios, was promoted to assistant director to Michael Bermond for *Poisoned Garden*—it was a British-German co-production you see, my first assistant directorship, and my first time away from Britain, and away from my mother and my family. The first night we arrived in Berlin, we went out on the town, and Bermond took special care to parade chubby, blushing me through every sort of district in which pretty girls and boys lolled on street corners wearing lipstick, boots-and-stockings, and little else. We went into a club filled with elegantly-dressed people at little tables paying varying degrees of attention to the tiny stage in the back, where a man in a tuxedo crawling on all fours sniffed a bouquet of flowers, carried a slipper in his mouth, and mimicked canine urination and defecation, while a beautiful woman clad in a sort of constructivist toga alternately petted and swatted him. Bermond said to me: "That's the great Emil Meyer, I'll bring you over to introduce you just as soon as his time's up and he's off that stage. We don't want to waste any of his money, now do we?" Meyer's *Verlassene Stadt* had been shown in London the month before and I had been completely struck dumb by it: it was like nothing I'd experienced before, not just in a movie, but in life! I knew it was clearly a terrain I wanted to approach, were I to make my own film, though I hadn't the slightest idea how to start my journey. Meyer was extremely debonair once upright and on two legs, and incredibly generous to my bumbling atrocious-German-speaking self as I tried to convey the depth of my admiration for his work while trying to internally integrate my experiences of his films, his easygoing conversation with me, and what he'd just been doing on that stage. He invited me round to his set, where I began spending as much time as I could. He was very kind to me, very generous and patient... he was very kind, you know.

That's rather surprising to hear, since he is usually regarded as having been a misanthrope, particularly, a misogynist.

Well, that's the strange thing with depicting and talking about things, isn't it? Do you do so because you simply like looking at or talking about them, or because you want to influence others to have certain opinions, or because you want to investigate and understand them better yourself? When it comes to depicting something like cruelty, even with good intentions lurking somewhere in the depths of your heart, things can get a bit mixed up, can't they? Well anyway, you know Meyer was very interested in witches, and the witch trials—on two levels, which rather contradict each other, now that I think of it. Emil was one of those sort of very aristocratic bohemian bolshie intellectual types, well, I guess that goes along with the generally being mixed up, but, he was interested in the witch trials for all sorts of what we'd call sociological reasons nowadays: were the trials attempts by organized Christian religion to purge dissidents and centralize power, or perhaps male hierarchies seeking to destroy problematic women, or corrupt small-time politicians adding to their wealth by seizing property and goods from old widows, or the merchant class exploiting the peasants, or the proto-medical establishment eliminating its competition in the form of midwives and herbalists...

Well, mass hysteria explains a lot of dark times in history...

Ah, mass hysteria... why sure, that explains the situation... about as well as saying that the cause of death was having been alive for a certain amount of time beforehand. But, after all, after you're dead, you probably don't much care whether there's an explanation, do you? I'm the last person to try to offer "explanations" of behavior and events; I'm far more interested in observing the complexities of a situation, looking at something, and just trying to... experience it directly somehow. I mean, I don't explain my dinner last night, which was an excellent experience; I can analyze some of the components—the wine, in particular—but I don't ever explain it. Anyway, I think when you're busy looking too hard for an explanation that may or may not exist behind something that puzzles you, or makes you uncomfortable, it's easy to miss a lot of details that would, among other things, disprove any tidy explanation you think you find. Why do experiences have to be "explained" all the time? If we rely on the explanation as a mnemonic, we're not really going to remember a lot of the actual experience—it will fall away from memory over time. You know what else is interesting about the witch trials? You know the largest-scale witch hunts of all were not only in Germany—not the stereotypical passionate and bloodthirsty Latin countries we associate with the Inquisition—but they also took place in the 1620s and 1630s: when the Enlightenment was about to dawn, you know, start the early Modern era, when Logic and Reason were preparing to usher in Progress... There were an awful lot of plausible reasons, unimpeachable justifications, impeccable logic presented in witch trials... why, there was a textbook to follow, the *Malleus Maleficarum*... and anyway... young man, you asked me about Emil, or, rather... goodness, that was a very nice wine we had at lunch, wasn't it? Well, to get back to Emil: yes: my picture, *Interrogation*, is an homage of sorts to Emil Meyer and his *Die Befrangungen*, which auf Englisch, is of course, *The Interrogations...* there's a lot behind that picture. Ah, yes, with his interest in witches, besides his sociological inquiries, Emil was also very au courant with all that fashionable Germanic pagan nature-worship of the time, which gave birth to so many complex things, from health food cereals to Nazi occultism and notions of "natural purity" I suppose... you know, I find it so fascinating that the Nazis Göring, Himmler, and Hitler himself were vegetarians, and you know some of the first legislation they passed, only a few months after seizing power, were the first animal welfare laws, anti-vivisection laws and things, even protecting fish and lobsters! I mean, in Britain, it's always vicars' childless wives in dumpy hats crusading for that sort of thing, not jackbooted...

That's rather... grotesque, isn't it? Those monsters, to be doing what they did to people, but yet protecting animals? Are you saying you're opposed to animal rights? That there's something inherently paradoxical...

No, no, no! It's complicated, isn't it? Grotesque, I suppose, definitely complicated... Like the United States expressing disgust at Germany's efforts to exterminate Jews, gypsies, and homosexuals, when their own nation was built upon a continent soaked in the blood of its first inhabitants... The United States filming its soldiers liberating concentration camps, while having put all its own Orientals into camps after Pearl Harbor, or denouncing Dr. Mengele's hospital experiments all the while pursuing their own sort upon impoverished Negro men, which have only recently been ended now in 1972, now that a journalist makes a fuss... Complicated.... So, Emil: he was also interested in, perhaps titillated by, all these typical romantic notions of women and nature and animals being sort of allied Dionysian forces with the potential to disrupt the encroaching mediocrities and tyrannies of businessmen's Apollonian modernism... so he was simultaneously bewitched by progressive socialist ideas and at the same time almost patriotically striving to invoke ambivalent primal forces... Well, I do not know how much he was involved with mystical or occult powers themselves, though I do know it was Aleister Crowley who gave him his first dose of heroin, but of course that would also have just been a fashionable situation in those days... so, with Emil, there was some sort of a fascination with the possibility that there was some veracity somewhere in various notions about witches, but... there's also something else. You know, Emil fought in the Great War...

Well, perhaps to get back to your film, if you could explain what it was that...

Well, I assure you: it's not a werewolf picture! My good man, all will be clear in one moment. What I was getting to was that Emil was a prisoner of war, you see, and so he experienced interrogation firsthand himself under the worst sort of circumstances. In his film, I believe he was investigating how interrogation itself is an enormously important tool of any large-scale tyranny. In his film, he set the interrogations within a finite context, an actual historical period, the known or assumed-known details of which ultimately can be distracting tangents for some people to get lost in and avoid the emotional intensity of the situation at hand, which is why in my film, I have chosen to cut all the mooring lines and let the concept drift into open sea, so that all that is visible is the abstraction of the interrogator controlling totally, dominating totally, by constructing a very particular framework strictly to his liking, into which all the details of a reality must somehow be fit, be made to fit, whether they are chopped off, or extracted by force... it almost doesn't matter what the balance of power was between two people before the interrogation starts, because once it begins, it is the interrogator who shapes the reality, who eventually has ultimate control, the final say...

Something else informs my picture, one of the reasons I do not equivocally give details as to whether the interrogator is a policeman or criminal or priest or god or devil, is because of those nature films I like to watch. A mother turkey, upon catching sight of her enemy the polecat, will begin to peck and claw in rage; she'll do this upon catching sight of a taxidermied polecat too, and what's even stranger is some person thought to see how far this could go by putting a tape recorder inside a taxidermied polecat, playing the peep-peep-peep sounds of little baby turkeys, and by so doing they then were able to observe the mother turkey greet the taxidermied polecat and attempt to gather it underneath her; then upon the tape's cessation, the mother turkey's rage returned. So, anyway, animal behaviorists call these seemingly programmed automatic responses to different fragmentary cues "fixed-action" patterns; once triggered, they always run in the same way and in the same order, and they are triggered by specific parts of the enemy, little details, but not the enemy as a whole. Male robins for example, will pounce on red feathers, whether they are on the breast of their immediate rivals, artificially attached to another bird, or left as a clump lying on the ground....

Well, all this is certainly very fascinating, and a bit... complicated! I'm afraid we've taken up too much of your time already, Mr. Wickwood. Thank you so much for sharing your afternoon with us.

V SOME MENTIONS OF KITTY DAWSON IN NATIONAL AND LOCAL PRESS

1. This week's Fresh New Face is perky ingénue Kitty Dawson, who's been handpicked from a Midwestern farm to star in the new Albert Wickwood picture *Man's Best Friend*, which the director says will make us feel a little differently about old Fido and Rex. We're sure this Kitty will hold her own just fine against her canine co-stars.

2. *Uncanny* box office receipts are very congratulatory even if movie reviewers have complained it's confusing and too long. Albert Wickwood is well aware that even his failures make money, and become classics a year or two later, and so he hardly waits for any reviews before planning his next picture. The word is Wickwood is now set to film his third consecutive picture with Kitty Dawson—and that's her third picture, ever. Looks like Kitty might be following in the steps of some of "the Master's" favorites like Helen St. Claire, who played four heroines for Wickwood. Perhaps she'll even inherit the throne

Maris Williams held—six plum roles for Wickwood in all, until her new prince of a husband insisted it wasn't royal behavior to continue in her acting career.

3. It's an "Enigma," alright: after three weeks of filming, Eva Martins has replaced Kitty Dawson as the lead in Albert Wickwood's *Enigma*. Kitty's spokesperson declares she is unavailable for comment and taking a "much-needed rest" at her parents' farm. Wickwood's office is similarly evasive. We'd heard rumors about some unkindness on the set of *Uncanny* last year, reportedly after Kitty protested that a horse was being treated cruelly on the set, and we won't even touch that gossip about the costume secretly soaked in pheromones and the attack scene in Kitty's debut, *Man's Best Friend*... It's long been whispered that Wickwood's unconventional working methods and famous practical "jokes" can inspire acute anxiety and recurring nightmares in his casts and crew, with Terence Peck evidently requiring the services of a hypnotist in order to complete the filming of *One Step from the Gallows*—maybe the Society for the Prevention of Cruelty to Animal Lovers should investigate this case...

4. "Kitty's New Best Friend?" *Daily Register* photographer Mike Herman got this shot of our lucky mayor making the acquaintance of Kitty Dawson as he welcomes her, Adam Hetherton, director Harry Ernst, and the rest of the cast and crew of *Night Watch*, which as all Lincolntonians surely know by now, begins filming in our humble town tomorrow. Hetherton plays a reporter-turned-detective, and Kitty his mysterious love interest. The mayor sure looks interested in Kitty, doesn't he? Kitty will be on hand to meet and greet the public on October fifth when she's the guest of honor at the annual Friends of Animals benefit dinner and auction. Kitty's donated a gold brooch in

the shape of a dog, with a pearl for an eye, which famed director Albert Wickwood gave her. We hear if you want to make a good impression on Kitty, you'll join her in supporting this local charity that assists neglected and abandoned animals.

5. We asked Kitty Dawson how it was to balance work, motherhood, and marriage to entrepreneur Noel Shepherd.

"Noel and I always discuss the roles I'm offered, and I only take on a project if I can be with my family." That doesn't mean this world-traveled actress stays within driving distance from her Sherman Oaks home, though. Noel and baby Rory recently accompanied her on the filming of a tale of modern-day smugglers, *The Doherty Connection*, in British Columbia, the Florida Keys, and Brazil.

Anyplace she wants to travel to most of all?

"I'd love to go back to Africa. I love the animals so much. I want my son to see them. I'd like to bring him there just as soon as he's old enough to appreciate it. I'd jump at the chance to be in another movie filmed there."

When asked if there were any types of roles she prefers, Kitty told us,

"I always enjoy the chance to work with animals, to travel, and to work with directors and actors I admire. But I'm really open to just about anything."

6. *Diamond in the Rough* is quite possibly one of the worst films of the year if not the decade, although Ross Carlton's toupee deserves some kind of award for best comic performance. A well-past-her-prime Kitty Dawson must have some big bills to pay, because it's otherwise unthinkable that someone who once worked under the great Albert Wickwood would ever end up in this clunker.

7. Sherman Oaks police were summoned to the property of actress Kitty Dawson last night after neighbors reported a lion on the loose near the premises. When they arrived officers found not just one but three large felines within the parameters of Dawson's security fence. An emotional Dawson pleaded that the animals had been dumped on her doorstep without warning. Her recently-AWOL husband Noel Shepherd apparently had not been paying the rent on the Cheranga Canyon property where the animals had been housed appropriately and where Shepherd had been producing a largely self-financed independent film starring Dawson and the animals. Dawson has escaped criminal charges for the moment. Neither Dawson nor the police department was available for further comment.

8. Actress Kitty Dawson has applied for non-profit status for the animal sanctuary she founded last year. Valhalla Valley describes its mission as "providing a permanent home for exotic big cats that have been abandoned or rescued from maltreatment, where they can live out their days in safety, comfort, and dignity, and where they will not required to perform or be on view."

VI   FILM THEORY

Introduction

One day you are watching the friendly detective—his sportscoated torso the scratchy, brown plaid stoic convexity of a cheap sofa cushion—talk to the sweaty and disheveled man who trembles on the window ledge as cars whoosh and blur eleven stories below, and you realize you despise the detective; it seems something about his tone of voice is infuriating, it occurs to you that were it you on that ledge, the last thing you would do would be what the detective suggests, you would find jumping the best possible option given the circumstances.

A few days later you watch the rancher entreating the mountain lion he startled from her fallen-log sunbathing perch, he drones and croons and beseeches, "Easy, easy!" as he backs up slowly in the general direction of where he left his rifle lying on a rock next to the stream that just refreshed him and his Palomino during their brief pause in a noonday ride through the desert; the sky, the horse, and the rancher's buckskin chaps all seem made of the same glowing yellow material, which alarms you, but most of all, you realize you don't want the rancher to be able to get away, you really don't want the mountain lion to be calmed, for as sure as you suspected would be the case, once the rancher reaches his gun and horse it seems he could mount and ride away unharmed without further action required, but nonetheless he shoots the mountain lion; you don't get to see whether she dies quickly or whether she lies panting and racked with spasms as life leaves her limbs, you only get to see the rancher grow smaller as he makes his way to the horizon.

Yet another day, you see a boy of eight or nine astride a horse whose hide is perhaps the rusty color of the blood-soaked sand where the mountain lion fell. They gallop along a dirt lane past fields of wheat and grazing sheep, as they approach a small bridge spanning a stony brook a black and white dog leaps out from behind a barn and lunges towards the mare's hindquarters, the horse spooks and bolts, the boy and the horse tumble off the bridge, and after a moment of stillness a great watery thrashing commences. The boy can get back on his feet but the horse just shrieks and moans. The farmhands approach, the flailing of workshirted arms summons a gun, the boy wails "No, no, no," and throws himself towards the shooter in the same manner the dog tackled the horse. The men wrestle the boy away, the rifle fires, and the air sounds like a length of silk being torn in two as the bullet shears through it, and the horse throws her head back one last time like she is breaking from a canter into full-on gallop towards her death. A man takes the boy aside and begins to murmur, and is it possible that he does so in the same honeyed tone of voice in which the friendly detective instructed the man not to jump and the rancher soothed the lion? And would you be grateful if, instead of sobbing into the comfort of workshirted arms—plenty experienced with, able to bear manfully, no longer fazed by, the gruesome and unnecessary deaths of animals—the boy wouldn't accept any of it, and would take off running down the road in the direction the mare would have continued if she could have?

You perhaps are a bit troubled or made uneasy by your mix of feelings for the detective, the rancher, and the boy; you don't yet realize it, but in fact, you have a skill, and you will in the future make use of your ability to hold balanced in your head all at the same time two or more ideas about a situation that might seem to conflict with or contradict one another. This skill will be discussed further, later.

Beginning: Defining a Group & Basic Navigation
- Defining a Group

If you are concerned with studying something, you will usually be told that it is appropriate to define a group of things. A grouping is really the beginning, an order in which to compare one sort of group to others, and if it is Things That are Made that you are studying, it is standard practice to group things by the maker, and so for example, it would be The Films of Albert Wickwood. TFOAW is a group that has already been considered many times by many others—this may comfort you, or, on the other hand, you might instead want it to be The Films in Which Kitty Dawson Appears, precisely because it has been suggested to you that it should be TFOAW.

It may seem unfair that when it comes to defining a group of films, the director is privileged over the actor—let us return to the names and spell them out once more to illustrate this point, that it is more commonly The Films of Albert Wickwood and not The Films in Which Kitty Dawson Appears—but in fact this seeming privilege may be insufficient recompense for the fact that the actor receives love, and the director does not.

We adore, perhaps even want to be Kitty Dawson as she appears descending the steps in a satin dress the surface of which gleams pearly in what we assume is moonlight. When Kitty lies or steals or even kills a person by accident, though we admit she could have been more careful or braver or at least removed her high-heels so as to have been able to run faster, we not only forgive her but also hope she gets away with it in the end; we feel a lump in the throat, a tightness in the chest when she is misunderstood or judged wrongly by the tight-lipped society matron. We never want to be the awkward fat man who sits alone late into the night making detailed diagrams orchestrating just how it is that Kitty can escape the would-be kidnappers by running through the crowded city streets full of vendor-carts easily toppled so as to provide a carpet of rolling oranges to slow the pursuers, balking mules drawing carriages that block intersections so the pursuers can nearly catch up, street-cars passing at just the right speed at just the right moment so that Kitty can jump on though the pursuer nearly at arm's length cannot; no, we really cannot like a man still so obedient to and frightened of his mother even twenty years after her death that he plies his craft insisting we, too, feel shame and revulsion and horror, at things that previously did not inspire those feelings in us. And even the director does not want to be himself either, he always chooses a handsome and slim man as his avatar, the one who enacts with the appearance of naturalness and ease all the scenes so painstakingly crafted, one who is fast enough to outrun his pursuers, catch up to Kitty, and who never pauses to think what his mother would have to say about his present course of action.

Defining a group is a beginning, and serves a number of purposes, but remember it is just one method of seeking understanding, through connections and affinities; it is just as easy to examine isolations and divisions. There are other methods of defining groups to be discussed further, later.

- Basic Navigation

Let us continue to use the example of TFOAW to illustrate more principles. Regarding what here we will call navigation: if you are working with TFOAW, you will find the likeliest, commonest approach of navigation is a sort of deciphering of various codes embedded in the films: a deciphering by means of any of a number of systems created by those who have pursued your endeavor before you, that provide what are said to be explanations for things like: the choice of an artificial leg for what the murderer uses to bludgeon his victims, the reason why the heroine is almost always an orphan, and why nearly always someone, villains and heroes alike, is disguised or uses an alias. In this deciphering approach, which is one of both codebreaking and translation, it is assumed that personal language always has some universally understandable equivalent and application, and that secret knowledge only need be revealed to be understood. In this approach, the whole structure of the film is broken down into tidy groups of sets and subsets of themes and factors, and when every component of a film has something it can be called, it has somewhere else to go besides being a part of a film, all the bits and parts of each film can be filed away in labeled compartments, like some children's activity kit that comes in a large box that can be used to reassemble the same thing over and over again or perhaps another or a few things very similar. It can be understood how this approach would feel comforting to many who might praise an orderly house as a virtue, or who might feel a better understanding of their illness by viewing anatomical dissection drawings prepared from the corpse of an individual who either did not survive the same condition or perhaps did but ironically went on to meet some other fate. When considering this approach, it is worthy to note that it has been observed of people fond of repairing at the amateur level for personal use their various household appliances—who disassemble and reassemble irons and toasters and radios and the like on the kitchen table—that occasionally when their efforts seem complete, they will notice a small shape slipped under the edge of the rug, and more than once the thing, when reassembled and in fact lacking a small part once seemingly integral to its functioning, still works. This happens sometimes on factory assembly lines as well, the finding of a part thought needed, and revealed as mistakenly so; we rarely hear about this as the part is always subsequently concealed by those who are judged not on whether the thing as a whole works after it has passed through their hands, but solely upon whether there is a part they left out.

With every type of endeavor, there are those whose primary goal is always to make the untidy tidy—and there are those who have other primary goals. In every endeavor there is in truth at least a bit of making the untidy tidy—but it is really up to you to choose to what degree, and at the expense of what other functions, you choose to be tidy.

At any rate, a system of any sort is but one method of accomplishing what is essentially navigation of terrain; a system of any sort provides a map that can be imposed on a landscape, so that clearly demarcated boundaries and familiar increments of distance suddenly appear where before there was wild country of unknown size, and instead of feeling utterly lost you then feel you can relate where you are to every other place you've ever been.

There are other methods of navigation to be discussed further, later.

Methods of Perception and Knowledge, and the Totality of Experience

Eyes and vision are privileged by many as being superior methods of perception and knowledge, and the person who experiences a film is usually referred to as the viewer or spectator, both those terms referring to the sense of sight only or mostly. The most-commonly discussed device of directors, a way of forcing a viewer to identify with and have empathy for a character, is to use the camera as if it were eyes in the head of a character, so that what is projected on the screen is similar to what a person would see out of two eyes. But we know that eyes are not the only portal of the body; and the blind who have no use of their eyes manage to identify with and have empathy for others. Furthermore, the technology of the film involves the machine recording of auditory as well as visual phenomena, nonetheless, it is still simplistic even to consider the experience of film as one achieved through a dual perceptual portal.

To begin to grasp the true totality of experience that is a film, it is extremely important to remember that the human body does not really stop at the skin: a walking, talking, peach-skinned sack of mostly watery substances occupying a place to the exclusion of other such sacks does not really comprise an individual, though we may have become accustomed to acting like it does. These flesh sacks we place such importance on, they do contain and separate somewhat, and what they do contain and separate is much, but they are not as impermeable nor contained by parameters as fixed as is often thought—for example there are microscopic organisms covering and inter-penetrating our interior and exterior surfaces living in symbiosis with what we often think of as solely our "I," multitudes of miniscule entities performing necessary tasks such as the catabolism of both nutrients and waste products; also, there are energies and frequencies of light, sound, and vibration that pass through us in waves, even particles of light from the distant sun travel through the universe and cascade upon and through our skin which is but one more region to be traversed by them as they continue their infinite anti-solar path.

Along this line of thinking, what is pertinent to the matter presently at hand is that the projection screen, when illuminated, is itself a permeable membrane, which opens into infinite space, which could be anywhere on the planet, or beyond it in outer space—-or magnified interior worlds, or altogether imaginary landscapes; and so forth. In the dark of a theater, in the oceanic matrix of sound and glowing flickering light, there flows an effortless titration between audience and film through and across the membrane of the screen—-the members of the audience are absorbed into a multiplicity that functions as a unified organism indistinct from its immediate environment so that, for you, as much of the you that is an individual, some of you feels itself sitting in your seat but most of you is expansively located in multiple planes and spaces all at once, "you" are mostly dissolved into the same sea as are the screen, the infinite space beyond, and the audience. This experience—-the film and the audience and the screen and the theater—-also produces an effect similar to a method of detoxification in which an object or an organism is soaked in a bath for the purposes of letting molecules of toxins be drawn out and released from the tissues by the properties of water, especially water with a high saline content. We could say that the experience of the film also causes the audience, floating in the watery bath that is the darkened theatrical screening, to exudate memories and desires; elicits shuddering resonances, chemical and magnetic gravitations, and catharses; and memories and desires float freely around and through, so that you in the audience cannot always be completely certain whether and wherefore something permeating your consciousness has arisen.

Basic Movement and More Methods of Navigation

As films are moving pictures, the study of movement should concern you greatly. Of movement within the film, the grandest and largest patterns are those that take the characters from beginning to end through and between various spaces and times; in each of those various spaces and times there are other layers of movement, smaller and more detailed. There is often an effect in which the macrocosm mirrors the microcosm, where the gesture of the largest trajectory is in harmony and rhythm with the smallest movements: notice how the protagonist or another favorite character navigates the space and time of an individual film, and watch for a symphony of large and small patterns. There is an especially beautiful sort of movement that takes place when a character moves fast with an explosion of flames behind him, managing always to be just in front of the explosion, outrunning it, perhaps actually being propelled forward by it; the entire film proceeds in this manner. You are likely to navigate such a film in much the same way as did the protagonist, and afterward you do not leave the theater pausing to consider what was burnt, collapsed, exploded; you go out and forward, never looking back.

You can apply navigational techniques of other sciences and practices to film. For example, *the archaeological method* would consider that the maker of the film arranges all the components of the film like a pharaoh builds a pyramid and furnishes it with unique and costly goods; he wants the structure to stand for a long time—long after he is dead—and the artisanship of the architecture and each precious object in the tomb is meant to please the gods and raise the maker's esteem in their eyes. You could proceed by dusting off and cataloguing all that you find, or by running out of the temple that was booby-trapped to deter robbers, bearing the most-glittering relic tucked in your pouch as trap-doors slam shut behind you, the entire structure collapsing in your wake as you make haste to pass through it. Another navigational method might be to witness the film as if securely belted into a cabriolet proceeding through a theme park populated by mechanical and automated figures in fixed tableaux. More specialized navigational methods might involve assuming the attitudes of private detective or psychiatrist.

Navigation and the Filmmaker's Endeavor: Devices and Strategies

No matter what your method of navigation, you can lose your way, and you can become confused and unsure of where you are and where you are going. But at the same time, you really can benefit from being at least temporarily lost. When people are lost they are forced to make or find a way, often making a new path; some of the greatest makers of films in fact deliberately try to get lost or to construct ways keeping themselves from going down the usual paths. Wickwood, for example, employed in every film a confusing device he referred to as the Gillycuddy, the existence of which he acknowledged but declined to discuss in any fashion other than a deliberately opaque one; it took those studying his films to observe the strategy and create definitions by which we might try to understand it. But whatever we think we understand of the Gillycuddy, it is very important to remember that Wickwood himself refused to quantify the concept.

The most common definition of the Gillycuddy, which we will take from *Wickwood: A Life of Films,* is: "A deliberately mysterious, illogical, nonsensical detail or plot objective chosen in a random or game-like fashion after the film's narrative is completely planned and constructed, not relevant to or needed for the satisfactory resolution of the plot, and serving only to grab and hold the characters' and the viewer's attention long enough for the plot to develop interest on its own; once the movie is 'going,' the Gillycuddy's job is done, it then fades in importance for the both characters and audience, disappearing without ever having meant anything."

A few commonly-cited examples of Gillycuddys are the finding of the gold Incan figurine in *Uncanny,* the pages missing from the manuscript in *An Incident Most Unusual,* and Katie's secret midnight walks in *Trouble Island.*

But this definition of the Gillycuddy conceals an alternate possibility, that the Gillycuddy could be understood to be a thing that exists first and foremost for the characters themselves, as opposed to being merely a device designed to assist the audience in hopping on a streamlined trajectory towards the resolution of a plot. For the Gillycuddy is the thing that Harry risks his life for in *Uncanny,* the thing that causes the Professor to be distracted and estranged from his wife in *An Incident Most Unusual;* the Gillycuddy is the focus for a character's deepest concerns and motivations, internal struggles, hidden desires, and to define that as having not meant anything is not quite accurate.

When Wickwood himself was asked about the Gillycuddy, he only and always responded by telling the same nonsensical story, quoted here also from *Wickwood: A Life of Films:*

"What's a Gillycuddy? Well, the story is, a man gets on a train and spies a strangely-shaped bag, inquires of the apparent owner seated below the baggage rack the nature of the package, the seated man replies that it is a Gillycuddy, to which the first responds 'Well, what's a Gillycuddy?' and the seated man answers that it is a special type of saddle used for the foxhunt in the Outer Hebrides, to which the newcomer exclaims that there are no foxhunts in the Outer Hebrides, to which the seated man answers 'Well, then, that's no Gillycuddy!'"

Recently scholars have pointed out that it is unlikely to be a coincidence—though no evidence exists proving whether or not Wickwood was aware of the fact—-that Gillycuddy is also the English common name for a type of bird native to Sri Lanka and famous to animal behaviorists for its controversial behavior in which it appears to assist other creatures of different species through elaborate means that seem not to benefit it directly in any way. The Gillycuddy has been seen to interrupt the tracking and interception of prey by predator by suddenly swooping in the vicinity of a sambar pursued by a leopard, shrieking and fanning its tailfeathers to display prominent eye-like markings that, were they the orbs of a new predator on the scene, that predator would be one so remarkably large that both parties of the original chasing transaction should immediately abandon their roles of hunter and hunted and consider themselves henceforth engaged in parallel pursuits, sharing the common cause of seeking refuge from an unforeseen danger of massive scale.

Fluctuations and Transformations
- A Case Study: "Yes, Darling, I Am Still a Little Horse"

So we can see that there are many ways of moving through a film, many types of movement and action take place within it. There is also a type of implied movement, between films: actors, characters, plots, landscapes, and motifs recur; and in the recurring and reappearing, what is the same in more than one place appears to have changed slightly, traveled, grown older in the process. It gets a bit confusing here, because in fact, in observing this type of implied movement one could at the same time define a group: a group could consist of Films in Which

Kitty Dawson Appears, and she would seem to have a number of consecutive marriages; another group could be Films in Which Different Women Are Murdered by the Same Method of Using Poison, and it could seem that a murderer beloved of a single modus operandi does away with numerous victims over time.

Perhaps the subtlest movement of all is the fluctuation of a character within a film. There are some systems that do not permit a character any deviation from a behavior established as normative in the context of the plot and setting, and any fluctuation is labeled as bad acting, poor characterization, or unconvincing dialogue. However, people studying film are beginning to investigate fluctuations as being a more naturalistic representative of character than streamlined behavior that efficiently produces the logical satisfaction of a plot objective; and, as strategies by the maker of the film, fluctuations exist as additional layers of meaning unto themselves.

Again, for an example we can return to Wickwood, and a film of his in which Kitty Dawson appears, *Uncanny*—one of the two they made together, the other being *Man's Best Friend*. In *Uncanny*, Kitty Dawson's character Lily Novak/Maria Dickens fluctuates greatly, mostly in the interest of allying and identifying with different animals. These alliances and identifications function as character embellishments—believable coping strategies for the character Lily/Maria, a traumatized and feral woman—and impart other layers of meaning to the narrative, twisting its arc.

This particular human-animal fluctuation really continues beyond the boundaries of this film. If you examine Kitty Dawson's work following her two films for Wickwood, she frequently costarred with animals during her career. The films she appeared in became increasingly obscure, but always featured animals;

some would attribute this to the mode of typecasting so prevalent in the film industry, where once a precedent is set a certain kind of person is forevermore seen only as a specific kind of character, the person who makes decisions about casting will never permit the glasses-wearing heroine's best friend or good sister to gambol about in the peignoir of a sex kitten, and it feels something like the incest taboo has been transgressed should the familiar dim-witted neighbor and sometimes filling-station attendant suddenly appear clad in a businessman's suit or a French chef's toque. The industry's mechanisms determine certain constraints upon the range an actor is offered: but, if we consider that an actor's resources within the artistic medium include what roles she chooses, we must give credit to an actor for asserting her will through what she accepts and refuses. We must assume for Kitty Dawson the pattern of animals, animals, animals was a deliberate artistic statement; and knowing that when she stopped making films she continued to work with animals, and created an animal sanctuary within which she also made her home, it is clearly obvious this was the case, that her artistic intent remained tightly focused throughout her career, and that she surely deserves equal credit alongside Wickwood for the animal-related fluctuations and transformations of *Man's Best Friend* and *Uncanny*.

In *Uncanny*, Kitty and Wickwood accomplish Lily/Maria's fluctuations and transformations through various methods: Kitty's skittish mannerisms often evoke the reactions of a deer mesmerized by headlights or a bird startled from its perch. In dialogue, Lily/Maria is constantly compared to various animals by other characters. The uneasy relationship she has with Mark—who knows some of her secrets and by virtue of this knowledge has power over her—is likened by Mark to that of a captive animal and a zoologist: Mark tells a friend he has "caught a fabulous creature." When Lily/Maria suddenly runs from Mark and disappears at the crowded racetrack, when she is surprised he catches up with her and declares that her "trail was hard to follow," but that he figured out what her "animal instincts" would be. Upon learning Lily/Maria has deceived him about her name, that she is Maria and not Lily, Mark refuses to call Lily "Maria" and insists on continuing to call her his "pet name," Tiger Lily. In a very complex scene, Lily/Maria finds herself at last unable to continue evading Mark's attempts to introduce her to friends and family; she seems to wear the mantle of general unease of a person who has woven a delicate persona-fabric that threatens to be easily unraveled should a person care to pick at any fact-strands. Lily/Maria passes off her distress to Mark as anxiety around not measuring up to his family's standards, but Mark assures Lily/Maria—-an avid equestrian—-that his father, a wealthy racehorse-owning playboy, will find her completely acceptable on the basis of her experience with horses, and when he makes the introduction he does so in a way that doesn't just mention his girlfriend's connection with horses but implies that Lily/Maria herself is more like them and less like humans:

Mr. Thurmond: "Is this a girl you've brought home, then?"
Mark: "Why, no, Dad, she's not a regular girl, she's a horse-woman."

Towards the end of the film the largest and most important character fluctuation takes place, during a phonecall crucial to the resolution of the plot: Lily/Maria refers to herself as an animal for the first time in the film. This could be understood as an end to her lies to Mark, that she is at last acknowledging herself to be what Mark has stated all along; or it could be understood as a surrender, an acceptance of a fate she is destined for. At this point in the film, Lily/Maria has deceived Mark with a story of visiting her mother, in order to see the abusive ex-lover from her past, whose existence she dare not divulge to Mark, and whom she must reckon with. It is unclear to the viewer which of her two lives she will choose, whether she intends to return for good to the first life and lover, or return to Mark. She deceives both men at once when she makes a phone call, as the lover thinks she is calling her mother and Mark thinks she is calling from her mother's. It is during this phonecall that it becomes clear, or perhaps she makes her decision, that she will return to Mark:

"Darling, I'm so sorry not to have phoned sooner," she whispers. "No, it's been no fun, Mother's had this awful cold, and I've caught it myself. I'm afraid I lost my voice, and I couldn't call. Mm-hmm, mm-hmm. Mm-hmm. Yes, darling, I am still a little hoarse. (Coughs gently.) I can't talk anymore right now, I'll be home tomorrow."

Lily/Maria of course refers to a physical condition that is a homonym for the animal, but at the same time, she also really says, "Yes darling, I am still a little horse," she affirms her identity as Lily, Mark's beloved horsewoman, and in the space of the phonecall and with this admission, Lily/Maria's transformation is complete.

So it is that movement and meaning take place all at once on multiple levels, and this brings us back to the beginning of the discussion; it is a skill to hold balanced in your head all at the same time two or more ideas about a situation that might even seem to conflict with or contradict one another, and to have this skill, you should see by now, will greatly enrich your endeavor and your experiences, not only of film. It is no surprise that we end with what we began with, endings and beginnings frequently have more in common with each other than with what lies between. In conclusion, a beginning necessarily implies an ending and often there arises a deep satisfaction when the ending seems to be one end of a rope that gets tied securely to the other end of the rope which is the beginning, and a strong, tidy knot is thus fastened.

A
N
I
M
A
L

110

S
A
N
C
T
U
A
R
Y

VII Some Conversations Between Various Members of a Small Party Traveling Together

1.

> You're not going to buy that little skeleton lion
> tamer? Now THAT is not your usual dime a doz-
> en Day of the Dead figurine, you're not going
> to find another one of those I don't think... it
> looks pretty old, too... and with your, shall we
> say, history, and all... and it would look so fab-
> ulous with all those other quirky little things
> you have displayed next to your bed.

Well, we just got here. I think I'd better wait
a bit before I start spending money on things
I don't really need. I think I need to see, for a
little while, how long my money lasts just paying for food and travel.

> What kind of cad am I, anyway? I should buy Señor Skeleton for you as a thank-you for that artist's statement you "helped" me with, wink-wink. It's the least I can do. You completely saved my skin!

You don't have to...

> I know I don't HAVE to!

It was good experience for me. And I kind of enjoyed fooling the snooty British curator...

> Sounding smart in my own monograph is a good experience for me, too.

(laughter)

> (laughter)

> Ugh, I can't stand writing those things. Someday when you grow up and become a famous artist I suppose you'll have no trouble...

> (laughter)

(laughter).

> Here... Señor, how much...? Uh, cuanto...?

> Tres miles, señor.

> Rory, how much did he say?

Here, it's three of these

Sor Juanas.

What's a Sor Juana?

(laughter)

Well I guess "what" is this bill, which is a thousand pesos, but there's a "who" component to this question too; the lady pictured on this money, and she is no less than a seventeenth-century Mexican dyke nun who wrote steamy poems to noblewomen! See, look at her wearing her habit and holding a little quill pen in her hand—how's that for a slightly more interesting currency decoration than our own nation's dead presidents?

I'm beginning to like this place a lot!

And sweetheart... if you accidentally buy a few too many souvenirs, you know full well I'm not exactly going to let you starve while we're here...

2.

Hey, sleeping beauty, rise and shine! I have some good news and bad news: Clive and Evan have finished making arrangements for most of the little field trips we told them we wanted to make while we're visiting down here; but the Whaleys will be joining us for many of them. They're kind of a drag to hang out with for too, too long, but amusing enough in small doses... anyway, they have collected a lot of my work, and that of Clive and Evan and their friends. It's sort of obligatory, I'm afraid. When I heard they were staying down here, I expected we'd do a dinner or two, but I guess when they heard I was visiting and planning trips to see the surrounding territory, I guess they thought it would be amusing to come along. But don't worry—and they will pay for everything whenever they're along.

Oh... well, alright... Do you know them well? What are they like?

Well, Terence is a senior partner in the humongous law firm in which the last two Supreme Court appointees were partners; you know, offices in every major city on every continent, their clients are things like corporations, universities. Helen was some sort of university administrator before she retired early about ten years ago following a stint at a certain clinic that a certain president's wife had just opened... the effects of which I hear didn't really take too well... Now, she likes to shop... They have a house in Saldana Cove near where Clive's parents kept a house for many years, I first met them one summer or another there. Oh, and Helen is a Coyne...

A "coin"? Is that some old-school euphemism? What do you mean?

(laughing) No, no, dear boy, a "Coyne." As in

Coyne Potatoes. Big old family fortune.

Uh-huh... a potato heiress... Well, that conjures
some interesting images. Ah yes, "Coyne Potatoes—Fresh. Natural. Simply the Best." But,
what are they really like? As people, I mean.

> They're like what you'd expect. Big collec-
> tors. They're well-educated, cultured people,
> they've traveled a great deal. They're not as
> conservative as they could be. I mean, Helen's
> basically a matronly fag-hag. I believe they
> have a philanthropic streak.

OK, great... I'm sorry, what I'm trying to tell
you is: I don't know what to expect, so I am
asking you for clarification, and in response
you're telling me things that only further ob-
fuscate matters. I mean... we're traveling in a
small group, in places far from home... it's kind
of an intimate situation, I'm just curious about
these people joining us all of the sudden... what
they like to do, what they find interesting... I
want to get along well...

> Jesus, just don't worry about it! It's not that
> complicated! What about your goddamned
> beloved credo of "be in the moment," and all
> that? Anyway, I told you: it's not like we really
> have a choice. Look, I'm sorry. It's not what I
> prefer either, but that's just how it works... and
> if you want to go anywhere with your art, you'd
> sure better learn to deal with it! But just calm
> down! It'll be fine!

3.

Hello, hello!

Oh David, it's been ages since we've seen you!

Yes, was it back in Saldana, or was it in San Francisco?

Actually, I think it was in New York!

(laughter)

Helen and Terence, this is David's, uh, young protégé, Rory, whom he met recently while doing a guest artist stint at a certain university...

Clive, you're AWFUL!

How do you do?

Pleasure to meet you.

Likewise.

My goodness, you're lucky to be here this time of the year, it's the best—spring break must be awfully late this year, then?

Actually, I'm taking a semester off.

Ah, I see...

(silence)

Well, it's nice to see you both! I hadn't realized you had a house down here, too.

A house! If only it were just "a" house!

Oh, Terry...

You two!

What...?

(entering) Oh, they've had a little domestic disorder...

(laughter)

You know how it is down here. First, we rented a place over on Santo Domingo, to stay in while we looked for property to buy. It's going so quickly, now this town has been discovered... Well, we ended up buying a place over near the canyon. The place we rented had three bedrooms, which we thought would be sufficient to use for the rest of the year while renovations take place. But then Timothy and his friends all wanted to come down after the semester ended, at just the same time that Helen's sister and her family were coming and...

So we rented another little place on Prieto last month... of course, not only did we really only need the extra rooms for a month at most, here you can only rent places for a minimum of three months at a time...

But I saw a number of ads for weekly and monthly rentals in the local newspaper this morning...

(all speaking at once) The LOCAL NEWSPAPER!?

(laughter)

Oh, so then, you actually speak Spanish?

Rory's rather, uh, earnest...

Guess someone here has to be!

(laughter)

The poor schoolboy's certainly used to being obedient, we hear he lost his virginity to a certain famous lion-tamer back when he was but a rough and tumble hired hand working at Rory's mother's animal sanctuary!

David, I can't believe that you...!

Oh, stop it you beasts, you're the ones who need a bit of taming! Don't be so tough on the little lamb. Rory, David told me your mother is the, uh, actress Kitty Dawson...

Yes, that's right...

Last summer in Saldana at the big drag revue

benefit for the alternative gallery, Miss Peepee la Poo did your mother in the big attack scene from *Man's Best Friend*, it was the hugest hit of the evening!

That was a wild night you boys dragged me to, though I suppose I could have lived without hordes of men in garish makeup and wigs grabbing my breasts and asking me how I got them so natural.

You mean, you *couldn't* have lived another day with*out* hordes of strangers grabbing your breasts.

Don't worry, they meant no harm; well, maybe just a little...

Why Helen, I'm surprised you even remember! I thought you'd consumed a therapeutically anaesthetic number of Gin Rickeys that night...

Gentlemen, you might as well be speaking Chinese for all that I understand of what you've been chattering on about! Your culture and its customs remain somewhat mysterious to me... and I think I'd like to leave it that way! Well, so anyway: we're going back at the end of the month, so we have not one but two places that nobody will be staying in the rest of the season, and then there is our future house... Well, the work on the house that will someday actually belong to us has so far gone as slowly as those big smelly buses they drive here...

Completely traumatic, it is! Someone working on the plumbing, the garden, the tiles, says "I'll be back in twenty minutes," and they don't come back for three days!

Or perhaps, with your Spanish, at least you THINK what they're saying is that they'll be back in twenty minutes...

Oh, David! You clever, clever beast... Well, each of our other houses, we had some idea when...

So yes, it has been so... traumatic, exactly. From now on we decided we are going to institute a three house rule. It's just too difficult to have more than three all at once.

Maybe David and I could take over the little place on Prieto for the rest of the spring, you must only have a few weeks left on it...

Huh?

You know, help you out on the three house rule.

(puzzled silence)

(slightly as an aside to Rory) The house on Prieto is just a rental... it's not part of the three houses in question.

So which domicile gets put on the auction block next?

I have never liked the house in Miami...

I'm voting we divest ourselves of Chicago...

But that's WRIGHT!

Oh it's "Wright" alright, as in right-up UGLY...

I agree: the thing looks like a tarted up chicken coop, long and low and dark...

Well, David, in the end, I suppose you're the one who's always "right" about anything in the visual or design realms. I am compelled to defer to your genius.

That settles it, then!

Can I get anyone another drink?

Well, you two should take a look at some of David's newest work while he's here. You can even pretend you're at the Mercado and get yourself a little bargain for the new house, even if you don't know exactly when you'll be moving in...

Yes, what is that we say? Hay un mejor precio?

Si! Gracias!

Muy bien, you two!

4.

What was that about? Were you trying to piss off Terence or something?

Huh? What are you talking about?

The house thing... the rental...

The house thing... Huh? Me? Trying to piss someone off? What? But... I didn't even understand... what, exactly...

Well, that's the understatement of the year!

I didn't mean to... I didn't intend to offend anyone at all, how exactly did I...

Well, well, well: you and your good intentions strike again. Isn't it the road to hell that's paved with good intentions?

But, I didn't... and... as far as trying to piss people off goes, you're the one who told him his Chicago house looked like a chicken coop! But he seemed to like that...

You can't tell the difference between those two exchanges?

Well, yes, but...

Uh... darling: maybe it's better for you not to try so hard.

But, I don't understand why it's like what I say is always wrong, when it's not. How come YOU can practically insult the guy and that's considered clever, but when I... Look, I just don't get what's going on here, it's something more than your average bitchy queen behavior, and I must add, the repartee is hardly very innovative... everyone seems rather confident they're smarter than they are... and, they're total caricatures! I wouldn't believe some of these conversations were real if I wasn't actually hearing it...

Well, I think as you get older you'll see that a lot of clichés have some basis in the truth...

...and you, you're like a totally different person! All the things we usually talk about, where is any of that now? Just a bunch of shallow small talk...

OK, OK, OK. Look... I can't really explain how it is being around these people; it's complex. It's just how it works. You're not necessarily doing anything wrong... It's just... how it works. Just distance yourself from it, OK? Don't get so emotional about it. Just detach, pretend you're playing a role. I'm sure you've got more acting talent than your mother.

5.

I'm sorry if I spoke harshly to you earlier. Truce?

Well, I wasn't thinking we were fighting a war, but... sure. How about, we say instead: let's make a fresh start.

OK.

(silence)

It's only been a couple of weeks but I feel like, since we don't have so much privacy during the day with all these people around, and it's been, shall we say, tense when we're alone at night...

(groans)

Fresh start, fresh start! OK, it's been ages since we've talked the way we usually talk... I think that's what I enjoy the most about our relationship, I mean, besides having access to your fantastic ass, of course...

(laughter)

(laughter)

But really, I truly love the way your mind works. Our conversations, they... nourish me. I don't talk to anyone else quite the same way. I'm really curious about everything that's been percolating inside your head these past few weeks. So why don't you sit your fabulous ass over here next to me and tell me everything that you've been reading and thinking about?

Alright, Mr. Fresh Start, but, I dunno how interesting you're going to find my most recent trope...

Try me.

Well, I've been reading about gift economies...

Oh... potlatches and all that? Like when the richest people in a society don't just show off their wealth but have to give the most gifts to maintain their status?

Well... sometimes, I guess... There seem to be conflicting views by different anthropologists... seems like there are different kinds of obligation and benefit. I guess I'm most interested in hunter-gatherers, who seem not to tally who brings what to the common table at the end of the day. To my mind, there's a kind of... egalitarian... erasure... of notions of productivity, of failure... of privilege...

Well, I'm sure they tally it in SOME fashion.

Well, no, actually, apparently not...

Darling, I hate to disillusion you and demolish your, shall we say, youthful idealism, but it's kind of natural that people would give something and expect something in return for it, on some level, wouldn't you say? Which, I think, you will come to see in time...

"Natural?" Did you just use the word "natural"?

What?

Well... do you really think... such a thing exists... if we're talking about people... Behavior...?

Well, yes, of course! I mean... how things work.

But people invent "how things work," right? They invent economies, they... it's malleable... there is NO "just how things work."

But, say, if someone gives you a gift, you can't really control how you react...

Huh? Well... maybe you act without too much conscious thinking, but how you react is learned, and reinforced by family and society, and...

Do you always have to make everything so complicated?

Do you mean, why do I see some of the inherent complexity in a situation where you would rather...

See! That's what I mean!

(silence)

So hunter-gatherers interest you? You think we should go back to killing antelope and gathering berries? Digging up roots? I'd like my economy to be based on something more elegant than roots...

You mean something more elegant than roots, like... Coyne Potatoes, perhaps?

God damn you...

(laughter)

(laughter)

Why do you have to be so smart?

(pause)

Another fresh start...?

Sure. Fresh.

(pause)

And even "natural"! And just simply the best, like a Coyne Potato.

Well, well, well, do we think ourselves too good to occasionally humor a potato heiress to pay our way in the world? But let's see in another five or ten years who's buying your work, and how pure you are then...

I'm sorry, it's hardly... I... And... it's not a question of... purity... I'm sorry, I don't meant to sound ungrateful, I just... I'd just like, personally, to do things... differently, somehow... if I could...

Well wouldn't we all? To some degree, anyway... But, I'm afraid that's just not how things work. I guess I'm trying to keep you from having to learn that the hard way, my boy...

Now, I think we've had enough unpleasantness for the evening, don't you? There's something I would sure like to do to you, the hard way...

See, doing things the hard way isn't always what you want to avoid...

6.

So David, we love those photographs we got last year, and I was wondering what you're working on now...

Do you mean, the photos you got from the "Nightclubs/Zoos" series?

Yes, yes!

Now, tell me honestly: you really love that project?

Why, yes, of course!

Because that's not exactly crowd-pleasing work you know, it's risky... it takes a certain degree of courage and, really, vision to collect that work. It didn't show very many places in the States... it was most popular in Berlin.

Oh, well, it's my FAVORITE of all that we have by you! It's true that not everybody who sees it agrees with me, but I feel very strongly about it! It's terrific work! I love it!

7.

Oh, here's a little something in this guidebook about that Sor Juana you like so well...

I'm not sure why you've decided I like her, especially as I don't know very much about her
aside from the fact she's evidently some sort of
a lesbian studies department postergirl...

Well, so, what's your book say?

"Sor Juana Ines de la Cruz, a child prodigy,"—
oh, that's why you like her!

Uh... whatever THAT's supposed to mean...

Don't be so coy, my boy genius!

Oh, please! You WISH... "Boy," yes...

Fresh start, fresh start! OK ... "A child prodigy from an affluent family, she was ineligible for, or perhaps liberated from, marriage due to her status as an illegitimate child of highborn parents."

Ooh! Spicy! Ahem... "After several years serving as a lady-in-waiting in the court in Mexico City, she entered the comparatively lax Convent of San Jeronimo. There she exercised her creative powers, flourishing in relative freedom, with a personal servant and an enormous library at her disposal."

Well, I could sure get used to exercising my creative powers with a personal servant at my disposal!

(silence)

(pause)

That's it?

Well... uh, there's more... "In addition to writing plays, poetry, and essays, she also designed murals for royal patrons. While she had an incredible amount of intellectual power and freedom for a woman of her time and social status, much of her creative energies were necessarily diverted towards flattering the Mexican nobility and the wealthy male clergy, upon whom she ultimately depended for support and protection..."

(pause)

Uh-huh...?

Uh... "After publicly criticizing a famous Jesuit, she was eventually forced to recant, after which she gave up her intellectual activities completely for the last few years before her death."

(silence)

8.

David, you evaded me the other day when I began to ask... so now I've got you cornered, and you've got to tell me: what on earth are you working on right now?

Well.... You know I don't like to discuss things too early on. But, I can tell you that I'm doing a project where I give people gifts and then document their reactions. The gifts will range from things that people really want or are valuable, to kind of banal things, to more problematic gifts that, say, a person might need but would not like to receive from someone else, or even outright abject objects. I'm working with notions of gift economies.

Fascinating!

Yes! And have you, uh, chosen everyone to whom you're going to give gifts? I'd like one of the non-abject ones...

(laughter)

Well, it doesn't work quite that way... well, maybe it could...

(laughter)

Uh, how exactly does what you just described "work with notions of gift economies...?"

What kind of a question is that? I think it's rather OBVIOUS, he's working with an exchange of gifts...

Good Lord, Rory! We're on spring break, aren't we? Can we take it easy? Waiter! Señor! Un otro, er... mas, por favor? This limonada is absolutely sensational with this tequila, isn't it?

9.

(Pointing to ancient carved-stone building ruins) Look at that! Amazing! Exactly the sort of thing I was hoping to see. Those faces at the base are so... knowing.

God! It IS divine. Of course, I don't suppose you can get a chunk of something like this for the garden, do you? Of course, I'm just joking...

Oh, Helen, you are SO terrible...

Yes, this is a very special place, isn't it? Makes you wonder what went on here.

It is quite something, isn't it? Though the guidebook says it's a fairly typical example of... its says the one at Mixitlan is the best example, both stylistically as well as how intact it is... plus in terms of how important it was ritually, the one at Mixitlan was used far earlier, and for a much longer period.

(peevishly, no longer bothering to attempt to convey as an aside but addressing the group as a whole) Oh, I see, this one isn't good enough...

No, no! That's not what I'm saying at all, I'm quite enjoying this, I just meant, I guess, if you find this one impressive, you might want to look at the guidebook, and think about visiting Mixitlan, which is only 45 kilometers...

(in high-pitched voice) "The guidebook says, the guidebook says..."

(in normal voice) Well, you know what, I actually don't really like to study too much before I

visit a place; it becomes a different thing altogether. I prefer to experience it first... fresh...
getting the flavor and feel without knowing its
history. History can come later; besides, so often you can intuit the most important things
about something if you set aside your rational,
Western approach. In life and art, I always defer to my intuition about things like this. It's
served me well this long...

Of course you know I highly value intuition, I
didn't mean...

Yes, that's the true mark of genius, of the artist, isn't it? Being able to trust one's intuition,
one's instincts, more than received knowledge.

I don't think the wonderful images and projects David makes could be done without great
instincts. Some things just can't really be
learned after all, I mean, that sort of thing... I
think you're either born with it, or not.

Fresh. Natural. Simply the best, huh?

(puzzled, ignoring Rory) David, I hereby crown
you our resident genius!

What do they call that, a genius locus?

You mean, genius loci?

(inaudibly)
Of course, that actually refers to an inherent protec-

tive spirit, or the spirit of a place in a metaphorical sense...

Well! If it's singular, it would definitely be locus, that much Latin we get in law school, you know.

(pause)

By the way, David, those "knowing" faces at the base of the temple are stylized skulls representing humans sacrificed not so many hundreds of years ago as offerings on the altar at the top.

(inaudibly)

So, on this structure you stand admiring, child slaves and captive warriors from outside groups had their still-beating hearts ripped from their chests by obsidian knife-wielding priests. The state religion decreed that regular offerings of human blood and hearts were necessary to nourish the gods from whom all blessings flowed and to whom the human race owed its creation and continued existence... Of course, the priests were members of the highest caste of their rigidly hierarchical society. Of course, the group of people personally supplying the least blood seemed to receive the most blessings...

...Horrific as the European conquest was, the culture that created this was rotted and imploding before it was finally completely destroyed by the Spanish.

Why, Rory, you seem a little angry about something that, after all, took place quite awhile ago, didn't it?

10.

Hello, David? Can you hear me? This telephone's a little...

Rory, where ARE you? Where have you BEEN all day?

I'm about 100 kilometers away. Listen...

WHAT? How did you get 100 kilometers away?

Uh... the bus. Listen to this, it's from a poem I found by that Sor Juana you decided I like so well:

No tener qué perder
me sirve de sosiego;
que no teme ladrones,
desnudo, el pasajero.*

Rory, you KNOW I don't speak Spanish!

But it's so nice in Spanish! I'll read you the English now...

Rory, it's late, and we have to... remember, we have to leave in the morning, Terence and Helen have paid for a driver...

In the time I have here, I really don't care about seeing a place just because it's known for its pottery markets, there are so many things I want to see...

But they're not going to understand... Shit! How far is 100 kilometers, anyway?

Uh, a kilometer is .62 miles. So I'm about 62 miles away.

Well, boy-genius, how the hell are you going to get back here in time to leave in the morning? And what the hell ARE you doing 62 miles away?

Well... I'm not going to get back there in time to leave in the morning. I am going to go see some places I've been wanting to see. There are so many places, not just in this country, that I want to see.

Do you REALIZE what kind of opportunity you are throwing away!? And the Whaleys will pay for EVERYTHING wherever we go with them... Do you realize... if you were to manage in spite of yourself to make a good impression on them, when you really launch your career... do you realize what...

Yes, but if we went someplace with the Whaleys, then we'd be with the Whaleys, wouldn't we? Even worse, we'd be going someplace where the Whaleys want to go...

I can't FUCKING believe you! Can we stop your little... uh... performance now? I am... losing my patience...

Are you going to explain yourself now? Where you are, and why you are there, and what you think you are doing? I suppose now you're going to tell me you're going to take a BUS all over the country... you'd take a bus all over the world if you could, I suppose, just gotta do it the hard way, huh, you and your damned hunter-gatherers...

Uh... OK, so that bit of the poem... I thought it was very beautiful... it was one of those moments... well, it's so much nicer in the Spanish, but, here it is in English:

"Having nothing to lose
brings peace of mind:
one traveling without funds
need not fear thieves."

Uh, one traveling without funds or friends need fear having a lousy, uncomfortable time. One pissing off patrons and successful artists who could help him need fear...

... uh... bye, David. Thanks again for the little Dia de los Muertos figure.

* From "Desengaña" ("Disillusionment"), Sor Juana Ines de la Cruz, 1648-1695.

VIII GENIUS LOCI

1. This temple structure once stood much higher, at its completion rising above the rainforest's canopy and penetrating the cloud aura, competing with nearby mountains to permit for whoever breached the summit a view said to be fit only for gods or their ordained human agents: it was commonly known that any unwise enough to trespass this divine law would immediately be struck blind, though after some time, some ordained human agents saw fit themselves to enforce a mechanical affliction upon those who'd seemed to have escaped divine retribution for their transgression. Each stone block was quarried two-days' journey from the temple site, carved and fitted by hand into a stepped mortar and block honeycomb that was in turn in places covered with a layer of painted fresco. What was long in the making was made to long endure, and its arches and steps stood level and stable for a thousand years, even through seasonal storms of earthquakes relating to the volcanic activity some hundred kilometers to the south. When the

Spanish arrived they began, like the eating of a pomegranate, to tear away at the temple's colorful skin and pluck stones out from its mortared pith, to build first a fort, then a church, then all manner of foundations and walls. Not only did the Spanish find this method architecturally expedient, far faster and easier and resulting in fewer deaths than forcing the natives through difficult terrain to quarry fresh blocks, but its other virtue was a sort of social efficiency, for the labor spent in building the new simultaneously desacralized the old, and the bastion of the indigenous religion was soon left looking like a carcass well-visited by carrion.

2. The small grassy hills here each mimic the form of the large forested peaked hill in the distance: a lumpy green mother and her brood. The mother is so shaped because many millions of years ago magma suddenly welled up from below the earth's crust, flooding the plain with a glowing, molten sea and pushing what the hill is made of, the former crust of older rocks, into a pile; a motion not so unlike the confluence of Styrofoam flotsam you see gathering into a mound on the eddy in the nearby river. The smaller hills are not properly hills at all, they are in fact where turf has covered over mounds of deer bones and antlers carefully stacked and arranged. When the herds were plentiful, each year at the beginning of the hunting season a designated animal was killed in this spot and its body split into two, the left half left as an offering and the right half consumed on the spot by the hunting party; any person who would have done such a thing lived very long ago.

3. The soil here in the valley is lush and these days apportioned into various enclosed pastures, embraced to the west by a half-moon of mountains long-tranquil since the ancient orogeny that formed them. In the center of the plains, a small arc of upright stones each the height of a person seems to mirror the

mountains, but its crescent is just a remnant of the full circle that was originally erected. From underground caverns a stream gushes up through a rocky depression to the east of the stone circle, the pool's cloverlike shape either befitting or perhaps begetting its long-standing reputation as a body of water beloved of whatever-gendered divine trinity is official at the moment, and capable of healing and blessing. People still come sometimes, climbing through farmers' gates, greeting various horned animals—the unneutered males, with trepidation—as they make their way to drink the water or couple in the stone circle hoping to ameliorate persistent ailments, relieve addictions, become pregnant; they may be more shy about their behavior when the sale to the developers from the nearby city goes through and herds of new houses start appearing in place of hoofed grazers.

4. Here, from high up above in the air it looks like there's a string of yellowish-ivory, black and coral beads lying on the desert floor: it's a series of small round rocky hills, circular caverns, and pools of some fluid the color of pinkish-red gems with many of the qualities of water—glistening; mutable surface, depths and borders—but none of the life-giving properties of water. It has in recent times been observed that migrating birds landing on the ponds died very shortly thereafter. People first started coming here to remove copper when they'd gotten all they could from where they had just come from; they searched for a greenish-bluish type of rock and when they found it, they picked and hammered with handtools, and applied modest amounts of heat and water and minerals in alchemical operations. Over the years, methods and tools changed and the amount of copper that could be removed with each innovation always increased, but it never increased as much as the need for copper increased at the same time; and so there was always the pressure to get yet more, and the gestures

to wrench the copper out of the earth grew bigger and more violent in impatience. Soon it was deemed there was no longer any time to pick and gouge out the ore, whether by hand or machine, so with the wombs of the mineshafts it became the practice to induce violent labor contractions by dosing the land with all manner of purgative substances that caused it to expel ever-greater quantities of copper. The land around the mines began to resemble the festering flesh surrounding a wound that won't heal. Eventually, someone made an error which no-one could figure out how to repair, and in a matter of days the shafts that had been mined for hundreds of years—and any small depressions in the surrounding area—filled with pinkish-red water that ate through the leather of the boots of men who first waded into the shallow tailings pits trying to assess what might be done. It was decided there was less profit to be lost in abandoning the once-fruitful mine than in any other option anyone could think of at the time.

5. Here, on a walk through the white birch forest in the late springtime, when this place is said by all to be at its loveliest, that elation stealing through you just now like a bird flying to its mate grasping nest-makings in its beak—can you actually deduce whether that quickened sprightly pulse you are enjoying arises from within you or permeates you from without? Are you responding, or is the place itself exerting its mood upon you? There have been a number of generations of birch forests here over time, they are not long-lived trees but do, on the other hand, grow very quickly and especially heartily wherever there has been a fire or other disturbance of the soil. How pretty their variegated bark shimmers in the sun, and at times from the path, through the striated view of trunks and shadows, the river can be seen at the edge of the forest, and then across its bank, the hay-meadow dotted with salmon-colored corn-poppies and doll's eye blue chicory. It's an excellent place

to walk to from the village with a basket of bread, cheese, sausage, and beer to spend the day gathering wild mushrooms; people have done so for hundreds of years, despite the presence of two possible wraiths one might encounter as nightfall approaches. The haunt with the longest history was once a local girl, said to have drowned herself in the river upon finding herself pregnant after her pledged-as-betrothed but unfortunately not-yet-official husband was killed in a hunting accident; the newer style of spook could be any of those brought here during the years when a truck would drive through the night to deliver a group of dissidents to dig a trench just longer than the line they would soon make when they then faced the trees, sometimes standing, sometimes kneeling, per the whims of the driver and the men with guns.

6. This place: let it simply be said that is not advisable to linger long here. Over the years there have been a variety of explanations for what causes a visitor to this place to become dolorous: ill humours borne on the night air, a contagious lethargy that creeps up through the soil from underground bodies of slow-moving water, or—in light of contemporary archaeological excavations—the resonance of the reportedly nefarious and ill-fated human activities from the past. Hasten onwards lest you fall prey to melancholy, a headache accompanied by sensitivity to light and noise, a weary irritability. The modern place name here derives from a Latinization of a word from a language that has not been spoken by a living person in many centuries. There is disagreement as to what it is said to have originally meant; there are those who are confident it has something to do with the cry of an owl, while others insist it is likelier to have indicated a preponderance of serpents' nests. This place and many others very different from it were once bound together through subjugation into a union of disparate realms whose one commonly-held virtue was to have been valuable to

the Romans for a few commodities: fertile cereal-growing land, bountiful hills from which could easily be dug tin, cochineal beetles, lustrous glassware, sweet honey, beautiful prostitutes, sturdy-shouldered slaves; this place provided abundant pitch, wax, and finely-woven black cloth. You will recall the Romans possessed numerous protective and tutelary supernatural entities, geniuses, to which sacrifices were made to ensure good fortune. Not just individuals but families, regions, countries, and ethnic groups, had their geniuses, as did physical places enjoy resident guardian deities, and the Romans often depicted one of the latter, a spirit of place—a genius loci—as a snake. The genius loci serpent here would no doubt have been black as pitch, its coils with the subtle sheen of finely-woven cloth. Did the black serpent arrive here with the Romans, or was there perhaps one nested here well before their arrival? The Romans of course tended to, when assimilating a newly conquered region into the imperium, absorb the most popular local deities into their own pantheon, which became the conquered's pantheon—appropriating and emphasizing any unique local flavors that suited their ends. This imperial strategy, of taking whatever it pleased them not to eradicate, and controlling it absolutely through administrative means, was pursued so exhaustively that even today, much of the Romans' structural organization, taxonomy and nomenclature—even the place name here—still persists, even so very, very long after the last Praetorian installed in the region issued his last edict.

IX   SOME PUBLICATIONS IN WHICH RORY DAWSON IS MENTIONED

1. From *Manimal Kingdom: How a Poor Boy Born in a Little Village Near the Baltic Sea Grew Up to Live in Paradise,* by Sandor Gebel-Wildenstein (with J. Levin). 1989: Ariel Books, New York.

p. 7: I will always be enormously grateful to Kitty Dawson, Noel Shepherd, and Rory Dawson. If Kitty had not encouraged me early on I don't think I would be where I am today. It all started when Noel attended a party where someone had a pet lion lounging next to the pool. He got the idea that location shots for a film he wanted to make would be cheaper if they acquired some exotic animals and simulated the Serengeti plains in Southern California. They'd originally intended to borrow animals, and began mentioning to friends they were interested in meeting people who owned big cats. But it was the early 1970s and there were a lot of "groovy" types around who wanted the thrill of exotic animals but didn't have much personal responsibility or discipline, and consequently there were a lot of large animals being abandoned or even rescued from abusive and neglectful situations. Before they realized quite what they were doing, Kitty and Noel ended up taking in a few "strays." Young Rory had a lion cub to play with in his Sherman Oaks backyard. When Tigrero was dumped on Kitty and Noel's suburban doorstep one evening, the neighbors finally started to worry and the authorities were notified. So Kitty focused on building a compassionate, secure, species-appropriate facility for all the big cats they soon found themselves in charge of. When I heard about their plans, through perseverance, will, and luck, I managed to get an introduction to Kitty and Noel. I didn't have much experience with big cats at that time but Kitty and Noel grasped how deeply I loved the animals, and they gave me a job.

The movie Kitty and Noel planned, alas, was never finished; but Valhalla Valley Animal Sanctuary was, and it remains a thriving place I hope that you, reader, will be able to visit someday. It is a great honor to me that Kitty chose the name inspired by my suggestion. You see, where I originally come from, Valhalla is an ancient mythic place, a final resting place for warriors; it is said there is room enough for all who are chosen... Humbly, I ask you: is that not a fitting name for a place of sanctuary for majestic feline hunters?

I worked for Kitty and Noel for about ten years, watching the cubs—and Rory!—grow up. And myself learning and growing, and realizing I had my very own vision for a life where humans and animals don't just coexist but are joyfully interdependent. Now, five years after launching my first show, and with the estate I am turning into Manimal Kingdom, I feel I have begun to achieve that vision.

p. 89: Some say what I do is no better than a circus. But I tell you: with what I do, there is no taming, which means to subordinate the animal to one's will. A cat can never really be tamed—they never obey, and never will. Circus acts have developed ways of intimidating the cats to—temporarily, and under certain conditions—perform; these circus people know their cats do not like what they are doing, and so their cats are locked in cages when not performing. The people are frightened of what the cats would do to them if given a chance. Me, I do not train the cats—the cats train me. The cats are actors and directors. I communicate with them, they communicate with me. If a cat doesn't want to do something, he lets me know; and I respect him. Consequently, everything I do in a show is based on what I have observed the cats like; I tailor the plot lines to suit what makes the cats feel good. The cats approach me of their own will, and anything we do on stage is all a joyous game. The most important thing is just to love. There is mutual respect and love, and that is why the cats I live with do not need to be locked in cages. They roam freely in my house all hours, and they sleep in my bed. Kitty Dawson understands this kind of life and attitude, and she has always supported me and my show. She even trusted me to take her young son Rory under my wing. Rory has a real gift for being with the animals. Five years ago, when he was fifteen and I left Valhalla Valley and launched my show, he came and worked with me over his summer vacation. He worked very hard and learned a lot, and was immensely helpful to me as well. My show has since taken off in all sorts of exciting and new directions, and Rory has also gone off to follow his own personal visions. He has recently decided to study art. Even though we now walk very different paths, I am very proud of him, and wish him all the best.

2. From *Contemporary Trends in American Art*, by Jennifer Gleason and Jonathan Bellmore. 1997: St. James Press, New York and London.

p. 187: This form of personal mythologizing, realized

through performance that references theater's origins in ritual and the transcendental/transgressive, is illustrated in Rory Dawson's early piece *Codex*. From the artist's instructions:

The artist stands and observes as four persons unknown to him previously, arrangements for their hire made through the artist's gallery, dig a pit of circumference and depth of their choosing. The artist's entire body of work to date existing in physical form—drawings, notes, prints, existing catalogues—is placed in the pit by two of the persons while the other two take notes, making a hasty and uneducated survey and description of what the pit contains. The four then douse the pile with highly-flammable solutions of historically accurate tree resins such as were used to ignite the sixteenth-century conflagrations in which Bishop de Landa destroyed what he thought to be the entire body of examples of written Mayan language. Each of the four persons at the last moment plucks at random one thing from the flames, in honor of the four Mayan codices that survived the Spanish conquest.

Dawson has described *Codex* as one of his "various attempts at grand restitutions, over and above the mere recital of facts." Dawson's more recent performances have included bodily mutilation and acts of physical endurance and personal risk, such as sharing a space with a live lion.

3. From *G.USH*, volume 2. G. Usher, ed. Undated (circa 1997), self-published, not paginated.

OK everybody, here's the second volume of G. Usher's *G.USH*, with an all new look. That retro version of the classic typewriter, cut and paste style 'zine was too hard to replicate again. So while I still love that old-school look, for a change now I'm making this all on the computer first before I photocopy it.

Our inaugural contest's winner is reader J. Williams, who

won the 16-mm film transfer to videotape of my dad's vintage footage of male dolphins spurning the females of their species in favor of some manly flipper to flipper action, because he correctly guessed that the G in G.Usher stands for "Ganesh," thanks to my hippie parents Margaret and Peter Usher or, M.Usher and P.Usher, as I like to think of them, as those terms just about sum them each up respectively. How much LSD does a person have to do before they think it fitting to name their son after a being whose father mistakenly ripped off his head and then in a fit of remorse replaces said head with that of an elephant? I would like to know, and then I would like to take ALMOST that much acid, but not quite.

Well, animals figure prominently again in this issue as our Favorite Freaky Fags this time around are up-and-coming artist Rory Dawson and—ahem—the famous entertainer Sandor. Check out their pinup photos on the back inside cover. You're dying I know at the cheese factor of including Sandor, you are thinking "G., he is not really campy enough to be cool—maybe he's just plain old scary, have you lost it?" But you know what, being that obviously faggy just short of wearing a HELLO MY NAME IS QUEER sticker on your lapel, and being so weird with all those animals, and still having thousands of mainstream middle-class Midwestern people go to your nightclub show and watch you on tee fuckin' vee, that is some sort of major subversive accomplishment in my book. I say, let us honor trailblazing even on trails we would never traverse ourselves. And after all, this category IS Favorite FREAKY Fags. And if you imagine him with different hair and clothes, and maybe before his recent surgeries, he is actually pretty hot.

"OK, well, who's Rory Dawson?" you might be asking now, because he is no household name. Well, first let me say that abovementioned father—as you may remember from my announcement of last issue's contest and the prize on offer—was a cinematographer specializing in wildlife photography. He knew this old has-been actress Kitty Dawson—who you may know from various drag renditions of some of her over-the-top roles—and now she runs an animal sanctuary. Well, Rory is Kitty's son, and he's an artist. And some of his performance art has involved things like sitting naked in a cage with lions, body-modification—really cutting edge stuff, pretty freaky-cool.

And guess what—Sandor once worked for Kitty at the animal sanctuary, before he ever had his weird show with lions and tigers licking each other, and him, on stage. And guess what—Rory once worked for Sandor, when Sandor first started his show.

Now, I'd like to push this it's-a-small-world/weird coincidence factor even more, just enough to make your heads start a'throbbing. Because I'd like to suggest something: let's consider why it is that Rory is considered the artist, and Sandor is considered the, uh, whatever it is that he's considered. When if you look at it one way, they do really similar things! Here, a scientific breakdown:

RORY	SANDOR
Does "performance art" with lion	Does performances with lions
Models work after shamanic practices	Shows have themes in ancient religions
References/appropriates famous works of art	Poses onstage in tableaux mimicking famous paintings
Does physical endurance & body-centered art, at times modifying body	Physical feats in performances; has been getting plastic surgery to look more leonine

And as far as the body modification thing goes, while Rory himself isn't getting plastic surgery, a Japanese artist has recently had various surgeries to try to make himself look more like an anime character... so that's specifically been done in the name of art...

It seems kind of random, the categorizing, when you think about it. It kind of seems just a matter of taste. Or maybe just class—like, art is something for upper-middle class audiences, and Sandor is so tacky; but then, what about camp and kitsch?

I don't know, dear readers, I can't answer any of these questions myself, they've been vexing me since they floated into my poor, troubled mind. So therefore this is our next contest. Whoever writes me with the best response to these questions, you will have your writing published right here in these pages, and if I decide I can part with it maybe I'll even send you my autographed souvenir booklet from the Manimal Kingdom. Lucky you, it's slightly soiled!

4. From *Wild Times: Notes from Past, Present and Future Spiritual Apocalypses,* by Peter Usher. 2000: Harmonyum Press, San Francisco.

p. 42: As a species, we must come to grips with the fact that we are on a narrow path between two cliffs: crisis and enlightenment. Only paradigm shifts can help us wend our way without disaster. Only through true seeing and knowing can we learn. True seeing and knowing is not always comfortable. I believe that in difficulties and mistakes, we not only have the opportunity to learn something ourselves, but we can also facilitate opportunities for others to learn. For example, I suppose in many ways I could have been a better father, but I can see how some of the mistakes I made have actually given my son the chance to learn to be strong and resourceful.

Sometimes, what one person labels a mistake another calls a breakthrough. One "mistake" that I was nearly criminally prosecuted for, was actually instrumental in the spiritual growth of two very special individuals I had the privilege of knowing quite a number of years ago. One of them at the time was what the state of California would have described in its court records as a "minor," a rather arbitrarily-imposed label—in this case, the "minor" at the age of fourteen was certainly more self-aware than many thirty or forty year olds I know... I can't go into too many details for a variety of reasons, but let's call the minor "Troy" and his older friend "Sebastian." Well, Troy and Sebastian heard me telling a story at Troy's mother's party about how, when I'd recently traveled down to the Amazon in search of indigenous cures for the alcoholism I had struggled with for so many years, I had at one point been given a healing involving the use of a psychoactive plant, and while under the influence of this plant, I'd been able to understand the thoughts of plants and animals. Troy and Sebastian questioned me at length, and I finally admitted against my better judgement that I had brought back some of the plant. Well, they wore me down! Let's just say that both of these individuals got me to agree to give them some of the plant and show them how to use it. When my longtime girlfriend found out who I'd turned on to this plant, she flipped out and very nearly reported me to the authorities. She could not forgive me for making what she called a "huge mistake" by giving a "kid" a "powerful drug." She relented on calling the cops, but said it was the "last straw" and left me. I felt remorse for awhile, but realized it was out of my hands. I haven't spoken to her in years, but I do wonder what she makes of the fact that both "Troy" and "Sebastian" are now very successful in each of their fields, are deeply spiritual people, and are each able to communicate with animals to unusual degrees. It's things like this that make me realize that I have to just surrender to a wisdom that is greater than my own, and rest in the knowledge that there is a higher intelligence at work in the universe.

X   FOUNDATION SACRIFICE

NORA—sorry to get this draft to you so late!
Those art fairs, one after the other, were totally
exhausting. As you can see, this is rather anec-
dotal, and I've still got to work up some kind of
verbiage about the new work, but at least you
can get started plugging in all the dates and the
kinds of details they want from my CV, and if
you can start going over my rambling prose to
make it a little more grantworthy in appeal...
And please remind me for the umpteenth time
when the deadline is...! Love, R

1. "Please provide for the Foundation's committee a narrative summary of your career to
date. Be sure to describe your training, your
professional accomplishments, and develop-

ments leading up to the project for which you now request funds. This account should mention any degrees, prizes, honors, fellowships, and institutional affiliations you have had or now hold. Applicants in science or scholarship should provide a detailed, but concise, plan of research, not exceeding three pages in length. Applicants in the arts should submit a brief statement of plans in general terms, not exceeding three pages in length."

In order to prevent my attached documentation from being overly confusing, it's necessary that I begin by clarifying that "Rufus David" is the same person as Rory Dawson. I took the pseudonym early in my career in an attempt to avoid being associated with the public persona that I felt was imposed upon me being the son of a then still-famous person; changing my name wasn't a very effective strategy towards that end, and so I took my name back, and in fact now, even though my mother's fame has long since waned, I deploy nearly the opposite tactic. I've found that in many contexts, even those in which you'd think there was little interest in B-movie actresses, still there is someone who is unsure and wants to ask, and their curiosity distracts them from the matter at hand even when it is urgent or serious; so, even in this application, I will be completely transparent at the outset in the hopes of avoiding anyone wasting time on speculation: Yes, it's true, my mother was Kitty Dawson.

It's completely illogical, but still, sometimes I worry he will find out one day. I don't know how it would ever occur to him to think of it on his own, as he barely notices me here and he certainly didn't notice me then. I looked so different then than I do now, and there were so many of us then, he never knew our names, and even if he had noticed me, how would he make the connection between then and now? But he would not have noticed me, he would only have noticed me if I had been one of the boys. He could only find out now if someone told him, if someone happened to find out I was working for him now, who remembered me from then. But how would that happen? I didn't stay in touch with any of them, and again, I look so different now, they wouldn't recognize me if they somehow saw me. I could have, perhaps should have, said something right away, when I applied for the job. But now it's too late. I didn't mean to conceal anything; in the beginning, I just felt like it was such a ridiculously tenuous connection that telling him would only make him think I was trying to ingratiate myself, and so I thought it would be better to wait until he knew me better and then it would seem like an odd coincidence, a bit of a joke we could laugh over—but that time never came. Now, if I tell him, I think the reason I didn't tell him straightaway would sound silly; I think it would seem more like I must have deliberately hid the fact for some useful or strategic reason. Famous people, they have suck-ups and stalkers and blackmailers and things, I worry he would get a totally wrong idea. Actually, I worry I would seem like the character his mother played in Uncanny. *I wonder, when*

you are a child and your mother is in the movies,
how the characters she portrays lodge themselves in
your unconscious as archetypes, how much movies
function in place of fairytales and myths to shape
what you fear and hope for in the world.

As for me, and my own career: as a child, I was always making things, totemic and fetish-type objects from things I found. When I was in high school and had a summer job in my mother's animal sanctuary I began collecting cast-off whiskers, claws, and naturally-shed fur from the big cats; I made little abstract forms, highly decorative, in honor of the cats, one for each out of what I found in her or his cage; I had them in my bedroom at home, it made me feel I remained intimately connected to the cats even when we were physically apart. I didn't really think about these objects I made as possibly being art until I went to college—an undistinguished state university where I enrolled without a declared major as we were permitted to do the freshman year. I suppose it was some general humanities requirement, an art history 101 in which you start the semester looking at slides of ochre pigment stenciled hands on cave walls and end it with twelve-foot high color photographs of human faces, you look at wooden figures in which nails have been hammered by the devoted wishing to implant their prayers into a deity the same week you look at souvenirs from when European painters felt for the first time freed from the need to paint representationally-accurate bodies. It was that kind of broad survey context of things made by humans that alerted me to the potential for sharing what I was doing with other people, the possibility that all the objects and attendant meanings I had constructed might be understood or at least appreciated by others—before that, what I did was always something I had the instinct to hide, or at least not discuss with other people. So, in college, it felt like art was the closest thing to what I was doing, that was a tangible, quantifiable, study-able thing I could declare as my major anyway.

Back then I was one of a number of young people wearing the same knee-high green rubber boots everyone was issued as part of the internship. There were usually about fifteen to twenty of us altogether, never more than three boys. We girls were as a group distributed in categories and proportions similar to those represented in my elementary-school summer camp experiences, which were less ethnically and socioeconomically diverse than my elementary school. I was one of the slightly chubby variety of girl, some of whom ate the same amount as the neither-chubby-nor-thin girls while others took second helpings or ate during the break time or in the evenings from suitcase stashes and brown cardboard packages sent from home containing frosted and sandy, powdery-sugar things wrapped in cellophane. The majority of the girl interns were neither-chubby-nor-thin, and there were some of us who were thin, and there was at least one of us who was thin and was heard gagging and retching in the latrine at the same furtive moments that the chubby stealthy eaters were unpacking their cellophane wrappers. And there was one girl intern who could not be put into any category at all—she was the thinnest of all, though she ate as much as the chubbiest girls, and she always smiled silently and helped out the most and never complained. I think everyone really, truly did want to like her, but for many she proved a little too unsettling to truly enjoy being around, exactly why it was so is hard to quantify—it must be said she was not helped in being appealing to some of us because she had a faint vertical scar between nose and lip showing that shortly after she'd been born the doctors had sewn up the cleft of a harelip. Alma: she was more like one of the adored animals than any of us. I did enjoy being around her, and in fact had to work very hard not to stare at her, knowing she would likely not believe that I did so because I found her beautiful, and even more beautiful when I imagined in my mind's eye what she would look like had she never had the surgery. I would like to be able to say we were actually friends then, but I was still too in my shell at that time to reach out to a person. I only had as friends those who reached out to me and Alma did not reach out to me, likely for the same reasons I did not reach out to her. But I have thought of her over the years, and recently have stolen some time during my work to do a little research of my own, and I am glad to see that Alma remains at the animal sanctuary, now a paid, high-level employee.

All of us girls, after our hay-hauling and shit-shoveling was done for the day, formed an ambling herd or marauding pack—our demeanor depending on a mystical concatenation: take one group of girls living in close proximity for one to three months; add midnight moon rituals that were for the enthusiasts a quickening of latent powers and sensitivities, and for others just the best time to share a joint; amplify with a symphony of numerous hormones cycling in unison and ever-more aligning with each lunation. Most of us were at the animal sanctuary the summer between high school and college, but some of us were mature for our age and would be returning to high school for another year, while others of us had been to college already a bit and would go back, and just a couple of us found for various reasons the animal sanctuary far preferable to college and would stay on a bit after the summer was over.

We didn't make any money working at the animal sanctuary, we were volunteering for a good cause. My mother, when she was the age I was at the animal sanctuary, didn't have such an option to work for no pay; in truth, when I was at the animal sanctuary I really should have worked somewhere for pay, too, but my mother encouraged me to do the internship, to her it seemed a real step up in the world that she could have a child that could work in exchange for knowledge and a vague sort of "personal experience" to be put on college and job applications.

I went to art school because I felt a vague but strong resonance between the objects I made in my private, religious-like activities and some objects I'd seen that were referred to as art, so it was a complete shock to me to find that most of my fellow students were in art school because they wanted to be artists, capital-A Artists, because they wanted to show in galleries, and they wanted to learn to make things—for they still didn't teach art as just doing things or thinking things at that time, it was objects—that could be shown and sold in galleries, which meant, things that were not too dissimilar from what you could go to a gallery and look at already. By the time I went to art school, the few ideas I'd had about artists— in retrospect, I realize these ideas must have come from movies—like an old-school avant-garde commitment to counterculture, nonconformism, rebellion against the bourgeoisie and its institutions, were all long-dead, out of fashion, or most complex of all, appropriated and made into a style and gesture worn by people who turned out to have more in common with studious business majors or professional party planners. I was told by my professors: art as self-expression went out in the 1950s; I was told by my professors: it is a logical and necessary progression that artists discard the outmoded ideals of critiquing the economic system in favor of acknowledging that they are an integral part of it; I was told by my professors: you are naïve to attribute agency to an abstraction, institution, or organization.

After just enough schooling to realize it was highly likely that if I'd been someone else besides the son of a celebrity—no matter how has-been—I probably wouldn't have gotten into the art program, with these little lumps stuck with fur and hair I'd made, me only able to mumble inarticulately a bit about them being highly personal as some sort of justification for their creation. As it happened, not only did I get in, but there were also a number of students and teachers who were always quick to praise everything I did. It was not too much longer after that that I changed my name.

In art school, I tried to apply myself: but there wasn't ever much information about the things and processes I saw that excited me the most. Artists whose work I felt a kinship with the moment I caught sight of it, like Clarence Burger or Jurgen Neu, seemed to lack any gaggle of fellow artist friends that could be collectively named as a movement; a disproportionately large percentage of them spent time in mental hospitals, might not have even thought of what they did as art, and perhaps even upon the event of their death their entire body of work was almost discarded until a doctor or landlord happened to think it might be worth saving. The work I saw that looked the closest to what I was doing myself was very often made by people from many diverse places that were lumped together into one category that some people might refer to as non-Western cultures; and it really struck me that so often this work I admired was presented to me the student or me the museum visitor in such a different way than most of what we looked at in school: these things I was always liking were also credited not to an individual but to an entire tribe, or as being typical of an entire region—the object-makers, one supposes one is meant to deduce, evidently laboring en masse, nobly sharing struggle and benefit and credit alike in the making of their things, things that did not so much have titles as vague descriptions alluding to their functions, which were never anything to do with being exhibited in a gallery.

So all the objects I instinctively resonated with, their makers didn't fit into any of the lineages of all those individuals whose personal family names and clan monikers we are taught to memorize in art school—the brand names, with whom we come to understand we should compare and contrast ourselves, who collectively spanning the ages we are covertly encouraged to see as one very large extended family the genealogy of which we are trained to endeavor to fit ourselves into. You know, even when the name of an individual of this sort gets lost he—for it is also always given to understood it is almost always a he—is bequeathed a posthumous Anonymous, or an honorific like The Master of the Bilberg Hours, or at the very least, we see the thing was made by The Workshop of Paolo Fermini, so that we are assured that an exemplary individual, the master himself, has approved an unknown-creator or collectively-made object with his imprimatur; and then, if you really want to get down to it, not just the makers of these objects are named and preserved, in the marketplace, the provenance is so important, the series of individuals through whose tender-fleshed hands the object passed over the years. And so, we are taught that the whole process is very tidy, though an artist might make a mess in the studio or on the canvas or in the gallery there is an underlying order and a sequence to the successions of hallowed individuals, there are inheritors of traditions, there are evolutions of style and method, there are logical developments and natural reactions against and understandable returns to what was loved before, fell out of fashion, and becomes fashionable again, there are neo- and new, there are proto- and post- and faux, and above all, we are encouraged to trust in the logic of what we learn is a smooth continuity, a flowing river that will never run dry. But it is also extremely clear that not just anyone is entitled to jump in and swim and drink at any time, there is some mystery around that which no one teaching the stuff really wants to discuss.

Now, some eight years after I was one of a group at the animal sanctuary, I am one of a group here in the studio; another group, another us. In this group, our demeanor is—thanks to age and the weariness of trying to get by in the city—fairly constant from day to day, that of a motley troupe of primates. What we are doing is still really hay-hauling and shit-shoveling, though some of us lettered chimps also get to go in the room with all the books and assemble papers, scribble notes, work on computers. A couple of us are unpaid and still in college or just out of it—doing this for "experience." Most of us have been out of college for a few years and some of us have even been here a few years and are receiving a small salary that isn't enough to support us really, but it is understood that we are receiving something more than just money or college credit or a letter of recommendation in exchange for our labor. We are working for an artist, one that has become well-known, one that has been described in art magazines, catalogues, press releases, and reviews as controversial, eccentric, and visionary—a unique star, a sun around which all else in the vicinity orbits, and we are to be illuminated by its glow.

When I arrived here in the city, just out of college, it didn't take long to see that it might already be too late, and at the very least, I had been seriously misled in my education. I had gone to an art college in a smaller city than this one, where I had been taught to make things. But here in the city, a city that matters, it was quickly obvious that real artists who really mattered, and especially those who were actually able to support themselves with making art, didn't make things; they thought of things to make, and hired people who knew how to make things to make their things.

The goal here for us seems to be, if you arrive in circumstances similar to mine, to make others' things for a few years, somewhat in the shadows, all the while at the same time, in your off hours, thinking and making your own things so that someday, you can be seen as a thinker. It is not spoken aloud but it is understood that for a maker to someday be in a position to hire others to be their makers is to have

reached a level of mattering. It is also understood
that this process should take place within a few
years, or else it is indeed really too late, and you are
too old by then.

Since so often I liked looking at a thing that
seemed to have been made by unnamed individuals usually from a place I didn't know too
much about, I began to at least learn what I
could about the peoples and places attributed;
I took a couple of semesters off and traveled.
Really, most of the objects I was admiring were
objects that had a use, a specific ritual use, of
which museum viewers usually remained ignorant. I saw that while there had been discussion
of Cargo Cults—it evidently being entertaining
to some to think that far away other people
venerated as magical and mysterious the parts
of our airplane motors and such—there was
not discussion of the fact that while our museums and galleries and collectors, by vener-
ating as magical mysterious objects from faraway places the making and purpose of which
remained hidden to us, were just engaging in a
complementary, reciprocal activity, little more
sophisticated and much more patronizing.

What I consider my first mature body of work
and what led to my first exhibitions was a direct and simple response to this idea, and was
comprised of found objects; I scoured thrift
shops and rummage sales for objects clearly
made or used in this country at some point in
the recent past, once familiar and known, but

which had grown obsolete and unrecognizable enough that no one I knew could guess the precise function of them: usually tools, kitchen implements, certain types of undergarments. This became what I began to think of to myself as Conceptual Thrift-Store Art. At first I was surprised to find myself a conceptual artist. While any artist's conceptual methodology arises shaped by freedoms and limitations, in the past one hundred years, some artists in climates of relative freedom and privilege have self-imposed or invented various limitations to generate a tension against which to play or rebel; using a palette of colors corresponding to mathematic equations, or writing a novel excluding any word containing "e," or sometimes the imposition is the art itself, as in performative gestures such as living for six months tied to a fellow performance artist. It's my conviction that clever high-brow conceits and precious obsessive game plans can inspire witty and admirably complex work, but if too abstract, a self-imposed limitation frequently insulates the deployer from her or his own personal struggles, and the end products lack a visceral emotional component, the game becomes a genteel pastime to busy the mind and distract it from solemn thoughts, it seems a more prim activity than playing outside in the dirt or running around getting sweaty—you don't even have to change your school clothes first. So I felt I got around this problem because the constraints of the thrift shop are not artificial middle-class mannerisms; art born of the thrift shop gets its makers' hands dirty, literally and figuratively, and though it may not cost a lot of money it cannot be easily bought, in fact, it requires something like magico-religious skills; the artist dowses and hunts for powerful objects, and like a shaman, must both sense and successfully lure out from hiding the right objects—an off day will leave the hunter empty-handed.

I began studying rituals more intensely, no longer just toward understanding objects I admired in museums. Quickly I saw how my earliest work intuited a number of processes common to various traditions of magico-religious ritualizing with objects. At that point I analyzed ritual in an abstract, language-like way, and was chiefly interested in commonalities between different cultures and, within the time and space of a ritual, the relationships between figures, movement in and demarcation of space, and objects.

After awhile, I began dispensing with most of the props, or would stage a piece in which I made something and destroyed it all in one process, and I came to be deeply affected by the resulting austerity, the act of sitting in a bare-walled studio much of the time began to influence me greatly, and initiated spontaneous meditative states.

Having gone to art school thinking I would make objects, moving to doing work involving found objects, I now moved into performance and the ever-less material. I began devising rituals responding to various historical incidents, generally involving the persecution and/or genocide of a group of people whom I had read about and, occasionally, whose homelands I had visited. In *Codex*, I addressed the burning of the Mayan codices and, by extension, sought to investigate the multivalent and irrevocable impact of the destruction of any store of recorded knowledge, how it is that something that seems as elaborate and entrenched a construct as a language can come to be expunged and uprooted from the very soil it grew upon, how distorted inventions arising from attempts to decipher unreadable fragments only hinting at some majestic cohesive system of meaning serve to further decimate and erase the language and the people. In this performance I burned every drawing I'd done that I could find, many of them I still had in my possession, some dating back to childhood scribbles, as well as some that I bought back from collectors, and a few that a long-time, extremely supportive, what many would call patron—and I would call collaborator—gave back to me so I could enact this performance. When I was preparing for this piece, I had intended for it to accomplish a number of things for the observers—I was completely focused on what I would evoke for the audience. If I had thought at all about what the performance might accomplish for myself, I suppose I'd thought I might feel as if I'd made some sort of expiatory sacrifice, that I might feel purified: intellectual ideas based on what I thought rituals accomplished. But what happened was that I was deeply emotionally disturbed by the performance in a way I had not anticipated, and I was physically ill for a good year afterward. When I had begun the performance and watched the first drawings burn, some self-portraits, I had experienced a number of intense visceral reactions, pain among them; I berated myself for what I thought was having some sort of emotional attachment to mere material objects, and pushed the pain aside, thinking I should let go of it.

My fame then lay in my sickness; aside from the usual whisperings that circulated then about any young gay artist's illness, it was suggested in certain quarters that I had created the performance first and foremost as a bit of a stunt to drive up my prices, which did increase, especially when rumors about my sickness began to circulate. But I later came to realize that in fact I had inadvertently caused my illness through tinkering with magico-religious methods I didn't really understand and thought I had not really believed in but had merely been academically fascinated by. But there are no regrets here, for the performance was really a rupture, a rite of passage, and the period of sickness that followed taught me what no art school could.

During my illness, characterized by fevers, pain, debilitating lethargy, weight loss, and swollen joints, which a variety of doctors diagnosed and treated variously and with many contradictions, I began having very detailed dreams about dance-like performances: there were very particular gestures, and strong colors for garments and light. I began to make careful notes and then replicated as best I could what I'd dreamed: the first time I danced, I felt quite energized for a number of hours afterward; it wasn't very long before I realized I was now dreaming curative performances, or performative cures. I began ritualizing on a daily basis, performing what I dreamed the night before, and within a month the pain in my joints had subsided. Six months later, I felt stronger and more alert than I could ever remember feeling before; the doctors of course announced that the initial test results had been misleading, it must have been merely either a virus or an allergic reaction, they no longer needed to name it once it disappeared.

When I was feeling well again, I stopped dreaming any dance performances. At first I felt a sense of loss and confusion: I wondered whether it was necessary to be sick in order to have the sort of revelatory visions I had.

I decided my illness looked an awful lot like the classic shamanic initiation, in which case, it was only a beginning, and that it was possibly my choice and probably my responsibility and potentially an inevitability to go further down the same path. I began to study in greater depth and with increasing acceptance of different belief systems various shamanic practices, and I made performances based on these, experimenting and taking careful notes to track my physical responses, turning away from activities that made me feel tired, caused headache, or gave me bad dreams. I set myself to various endurance projects, beginning with *Land, Air, Sea: Loxodonta africanus, Falco peregrinus, Tursiops truncatus*, where I ate, moved, and slept for set periods of time according to the schedules and rhythms of a sequence of animals other than my own species; for each segment, I constructed an environment for myself that included the primary element that was home to the corresponding animal—the elephant, I filled the room with mud; the falcon, I was suspended in a harness; the dolphin, I remained in a tank of water. I observed the other creature in her or his environment on a closed-circuit monitor and followed their activities as best I could, assistants observed us as we slept and awakened me if the other creature awakened before me. In *Two Ways About It,* I lived in a cell connected to a lion's pen by a two-way mirror through which the lion could observe me but which only reflected back to me my own image; I took a vow to stay—as long as it took—until I no longer saw myself but saw the, or a, lion. This took a little over three months; I still do not understand whether I saw the lion, a lion, or myself as a lion, and I do not think knowing that is really of any importance, the doing of it all was the point.

During *Two Ways About It* I began to recognize that I had intense anger at my mother. I realized the early fetish-object type work was in many ways various intuited methods of shamanic acquisition of animal powers, in part as a result of a child wanting to become what my mother seemed to love more than she loved me, the animals on the sanctuary. I did not want to be angry at my mother. I had never before been able to recognize my anger for what it was since my mother was such a fragile creature, always suffering, seemingly incapable of being an active agent of anything that could cause rage: my mother was someone to love, to help, to pity, to protect, and it felt inhuman, impossible, also to feel anger at a person inspiring those gentle qualities. At first when I determined I was so angry I turned it against myself, blamed myself for feeling such an emotion, thinking that a person so concerned as I am with empathy and compassion ought to be able to let go of such a violent thing as anger that seems at first just to be destructive, pain-inducing force... and then I considered how I had really made my illness—a thing I hadn't consciously asked for that can also seem only to be destructive, pain-inducing—a major transformation, a teaching, something I was actually in the end grateful for and considered a gift. So I set about looking at this anger I had, trying to understand it, wanting to catabolize it into base elements so I could pick out the useful materials, and to be transformed by the process of transmutation.

I moved from performance to video at this stage: the immaterial was captured, kinetic time/space/energy congealing somewhat to matter in the form of documentation. I started by watching all of my mother's films in an endurance-project fashion. I watched them over and over again: first in chronological sequence, and then, I would queue up a sequence based on a theme I detected and watch those films all in one sitting. All the films where she had a secret identity; all the films where she was brunette; all the films where she gets killed.

My viewing methodologies ultimately caused me to begin to assemble footage in different patterns, creating my own narratives. *Yes, Mother I am Still a Little Horse* is a montage of clips from various films in which all dialogue is deleted except that in which my mother compares herself or is compared by other characters to animals, or animals are shown, mentioned or implied. It becomes an incantation, she seems to have been summoning during the fifteen years of her acting career her ultimate role, a resident of the animal sanctuary.

I'd wanted to avoid the subject of Albert Wickwood, as so many artists have already found him rich source material, so much has already been said about him, and the types who typically become completely enamored of him are lovers of theoretical systems, for he made a very specific type of closed universe to which many systems and schools of thought can be applied in a very tidy fashion: psychoanalysis, structuralism, feminist film theory, cultural studies, and so on. Not an intellectual, I felt over my head in trying to deal with Wickwood in an appropriate and meaningful way, given the numerous substantial precedents for how he had already been looked at. But in the end it was unavoidable due to my personal connection; my mother would never speak about him, but it was evident in watching the two films she made for him, *Man's Best Friend* and *Uncanny*, her eyes—her own eyes, not the carefully-played eyes of a character—are so frightened! So then I found myself watching all of the Wickwood films I could, not just the two with my mother; this began a three-year period during which I returned to art concerned with the production of objects, on a more complex scale than ever before, utilizing assistants and fabricators. I began work on the major video and sculpture installation project *Foundation Sacrifice*.

I became one of the makers. There weren't always so many makers in recent times, for quite a number of years, it wasn't at all the fashion to present yourself as an artist associated with object-making, art for awhile was all about allegedly intangible, transient ephemeral temporal moments of interaction with audiences or environments. But always, there was documentation; so in the end it was not matter at all that was rejected, while pretending to escape materiality that action was actually turned into an easily repeatable gesture and not an actual practice:

there were plenty of installation shots, videos, stills, sketches, and maquettes that could be handily sold in galleries and displayed in the mausoleum-museums, and which always referred back to the artist, the art, and the institutions of art. If there was ever any attempt by an artist to try to make or do something that actually mattered outside itself or outside the bounds of its carefully circumscribed enclosure where its existing audience already knew to come look for it, it was ignored or ridiculed. From time to time, it's been briefly fashionable to make something that seems to mean or say something that pertains to the world outside the artist and artworld, but usually it just looks like it does, and whatever meaning it carries does not travel any further beyond the gallery walls.

We makers seem to sense there are other merits besides the pay in being makers; many of us look down on those in our situation who take other jobs not related to art. I quickly learned that there is actually one major risk in being a maker: if we are spotted and identified as makers, by certain functionaries in the artworld, say, if a curator visits the studio to see the artist—the official artist, who really matters—and sees us there kneeling on the floor, at the computer, wrapping something up, it is all over; the taint of being a maker will now cling fast to us, we may have seen that same curator before at openings and parties, perhaps even been smiled at, or our schmoozing patiently tolerated because we were smart in choosing our clothes that we couldn't really afford but convinced ourselves were necessary

SARAH

FALKNER

for the task, because we may have been mistaken by the curator for being an individual who might matter, but after we have been identified with making things, taking care of things, by putting things away in an orderly fashion, and especially moving things using the service elevator, the very substance of our being changes, we are now one of many, we are not an individual, we are a category, we are a subset under the heading of artist's studio, we are planets that orbit a star, and planets do not become stars and emit their own brightness but remain reflective and tangential. When next we see the same curator at an opening, her or his gaze can pass right through our now-realized nonexistentness as it searches for someone really worthy of acknowledgement.

Even if we are successful in concealing our labor and status from those we must, there is actually an even larger problem. When we go home at night we have been looking at and making someone else's art all day, and so it is a funny thing to quickly put together some dinner and then try to make some of our own art in the few hours before we go to sleep, or perhaps on our day off to sit in our own studio. How can our hands even tell the difference sometimes, between his art and our own, when we are holding a brush, pouring a mold, setting coordinate points for a vector?

It's interesting how art that matters now is so ambitious in scope and scale that it must be made according to the plan of one person, and then executed by numerous hands; yet just what is it that I still make in the evenings and days off, all by myself? Or what is it that my friends and I make together, without someone directing us or paying us? Some of us want to avoid the system that decides what matters and what doesn't, work outside it, avoid the topic altogether; but in truth, not one of us can really convince ourselves somehow that what we have in our studios and houses and heads actually matters even to ourselves as much as some of what we see in the galleries, the museums, the magazines.

Do you know how when many an ancient building of great importance is excavated, animal and human remains are found in the walls and beneath the cornerstone and foundation? Various ancient peoples made foundation sacrifices, both to propitiate the spirit of the place in which building operations are about to disturb, and to appropriate various attributes on behalf of the structure and its guardian spirits; the more costly the building, the more numerous and valuable the sacrifices. In every Albert Wickwood film there is elaborate artifice employed towards making an intricate structure, and each film is an expensive castle in which there has been at least one beautiful woman sacrificed so that the gods will ensure the walls stand firm.

I enjoy and respect the scholars who read within Wickwood's films subversive narratives, critiquing the first wave of criticism, arguing, for example, that he had to represent patriarchal institutionalized violence in order to critique it—but, in the end, sometimes a cigar is just a cigar, and sometimes a mother-fixated misogynist is just a mother-fixated misogynist, so in this case, I could not agree with such a fresh reading myself in light of what seemed to be my mother's experience; the cliché had as its basis truth.

As I meditated with the Wickwood material it seemed to me the cruelty he both represented and deployed in the service of making his representations was first and foremost the result of the intense anger he felt towards his own mother, which he'd never managed to work out completely; I used this as a lens through which to view my own work and its relationship to my relationship with my mother. I realized I had appropriated my mother for my own ends just as surely as any Victorian Orientalist painter depicts an exotic "other."

As this period was coming to artistic fruition, my mother was diagnosed with breast cancer. I sought to repair my relationship with her, moved back to the animal sanctuary, eventually becoming extremely involved in her care, researching all manner of alternative therapies and helping her negotiate her dealings with the medical-industrial complex. During the eighteen months I lived with my mother, the final pieces from the *Foundation Sacrifice* project were completed in the studio.

Rory seems like he tries to be different than a lot of artists in how he relates to the artworld, and cer-

tainly his art has at times critiqued various aspects of it. But in the end, he's still the artist, and we're still the makers.

Even though we're the makers and know about making things, sometimes the artist overrides our judgment and experience in the thrall of innovation, novelty, artistic licence. Here it gets really tricky: sometimes there are very good reasons why no one ever made things out of certain materials before, why no one tried to do certain things before. When Cynthia worked for Kenneth Geary, she made sure to wear gloves when she was coating a large group of small wax figurines with pigments Kenneth had collected himself in the desert; nonetheless her fingernails began to grow out from the quick a distinctly bluish hue. "Well that can't be good! After this show we'll stop using them," Kenneth told her, patting her shoulder. Before Jacob worked for Rory, he worked for Kinzu Yamada, when Yamada was doing massive kinetic sculptures praised for seeming to defy gravity; in the artist's studio, the assistants struggled with prototypes that were often quite obedient to the laws of physics, and Jacob had the privilege of receiving a concussion, various bloody gashes, and two broken fingers from "I ROBOT 497," a piece that would later go on to fetch a record price for a Yamada at auction before it was whisked off to the collector's warehouse where now, two years on, it still sits in its crate. When Jacob regained consciousness on the studio floor the first thing he did was stop a fellow assistant from calling an ambulance—"Do you know how much that costs if you don't have health insurance?" Yamada, arriving on the scene having been summoned from his lunch by a third assistant, pulled a twenty out of his wallet with great flourish and told them to take a taxi to the nearest hospital, since after all they were working with salvaged, rusting metal. "Tetanus shot, that's what you need," he said sagely. "Oh, and don't forget the taxi receipt," he called after them in the stairwell.

Compared to many jobs, there is quite a lot to enjoy: we wear what we like, we meet interesting people, we can often arrange our schedules to be convenient to some other things we have to do. Makers are sometimes paid fairly well for an hourly wage, but none of us has any kind of security or benefits. We are assured that it's a trade-off to accept the conditions as they are so as to have a flexible schedule, so that we might make our own art instead of working in an office like everybody else who rides the subway during rush hour. It is explained to us that the artist would love to offer us health insurance if only he could afford it, but the cost is simply prohibitive; he can barely afford to do the projects he does that we're hired for in the first place.

None of the gold dust clinging to the stars we orbit ever seems to rub off on us, no matter how close to them we work. There is something else that keeps us doing these jobs.

After my mother's death a year ago, I began a piece I conceived of as a memorial tribute to her. When I began, I thought I was both working with my own grief and also in some small way contributing to righting some of the wrongs done my mother, perhaps even done all women by the patriarchal medical system. But in the end I realized I would be making a foundation sacrifice of my own. To make the project at all was to make a vanishing people of my mother, a species going extinct. I had the arrogance of a missionary, a representative of a conquering colonizing nation, to take ownership of how and what of her memory and experience ought to be classified, represented, preserved.

I abandoned the piece about my mother's death and have not completed any major projects since that time.

I now seek funds to support research for my nascent body of work investigating the relationship between art, ritual, and healing practices.

[NORA—more to come here, also, feel free to take a stab at it yourself...!]

The first research I did for Rory centered on sacrifice, especially human. Certain writers on the topic have said that it was understood to be a great honor, a sign of great nobility and courage; or there were special favors bestowed: a period of time beforehand of great feasting and fêtes in which the one to be sacrificed was a type of king. The sacrificed was holy, the sacrificers identified with the sacrificed, they were a dialectic, they merged destinies. The sacrificed, in many societies, were said to have gone proudly and willingly, knowing that they served a purpose greater than themselves.

But I suspect that there is a dynamic at work with many of these writers who describe the worthiness and nobility of the sacrifice, I suspect that the writer is to the priest and the priest to the sacrificed as is the curator to the artist and the artist to the maker. I suspect there were always ropes affixing the sacrificed to the altars, that no one preserved their frayed and clawed-at remains as evidence that would need to be explained.

I have been thinking of Alma a lot lately, checking out what she does at the animal sanctuary; in this year's annual members' newsletter she notes that her chief mentor and thesis advisor, Edna Garth, has designed a number of structures used in commercial animal husbandry. By having some empathy for and understanding of the emotional and psychological lives of some animals and, without addressing the issue of whether or not animals actually should or should not live and/or die at the whim of humans, Edna has made it her vocation to greatly reduce the amount of suffering endured by animals living and dying on large automated farms. Previous structures frequently caused animals to panic and balk while queued up to go single file through routine actions and movements, often injuring themselves and their kin. With the new inventions, the architectonics and visual stimuli are geared towards the experience of quadrupeds with species-specific sensory apparatuses; a frontal-eyed biped with feeble and scanty olfactory nerves walking through a chute he has built himself may find nothing alarming during his journey, but a creature whose spine is parallel to the earth will see a different interplay of light and shadow than does the human, a creature who can find fresh grass by its scent on the wind will find the odor of fresh paint intolerable, in any case, a space comfortable and familiar to a human is likely a space uncomfortable and unfamiliar to another species, the human animal hears such a small range of Hz frequencies, sees such limited sections of the electromagnetic spectrum compared to many other species, and misses out altogether on conscious apprehension of various radiations and chemical presences, it is easy for there to be many factors overlooked by a human making a place meant to be comfortable for an animal. The purpose of the new chutes is not to fool any creature into thinking they are going anywhere else than where they are, it is just to make them more comfortable. As intelligent and sentient as Alma and her mentor and countless others have demonstrated nonhuman animals to be, it hardly seems the animals are no less aware of what faces them on the other end of the chute than were their balking kin, but their journey takes place in spaces that feel familiar, and that seems to be what is important to them; it could be said to be a very different paradigm that the one in which humans privilege any end over whatever means to it. With these new inventions, their step-by-step journeys feeling familiar, animals will go calmly through the newly-designed structure to be immersed over their heads in tick dip, to be restrained for veterinary procedures, even to be stunned to unconsciousness by *an electric bolt pistol or blunt trauma to the head just before having their throats slit.*

I don't blame Rory for how things are as much as I would most artists; on certain levels he tries to be the best he can, he's aware of inequity in the artworld, he tries to address it in the ways it has occurred to him, but he makes a common error in thinking that since as a gay man he can be considered a member of a group that has been oppressed, he has some sort of exemption from ever being considered oppressive himself. I believe he thinks he can participate in various institutions, the museum and gallery system, art school, the market, and subvert or improve them; but from his position he cannot see that he is in fact one of many bricks in the wall of the temple of art; he helps build, maintain and support these oppressive structures—and in turn he's held in place himself by those structures. He's tried to make the structures he erects more humane, but whether or not they have gentler edges or diverse ornamentation, in the end they still serve the same purpose.

It seems to me the only hope for things ever to be different enough, really fair enough, must surely lie in demolishing the existing structures. No more foundation sacrifices, but instead sacrifices of the structures all the way down to the foundations. Then maybe something altogether different can be built from the ground up, with no people or animals buried under it.

XI   Some Scenarios Which Kitty Dawson Has Rehearsed

1. Falling is very lovely and graceful, in a general sense; the gesture of a body as an arc careening in descent, when viewed from a distance, is compelling and hypnotic. Whether you jump, are pushed, or have an accident, after the first few seconds, the degree of your own agency in your departure from the heights loses all relevance, for you the wingless, flightless creature, are completely passive once borne in the medium of air. The forces of gravity, velocity, and air currents sculpt the shape your body makes in space as it falls, you are transformed by your environment like a stone is polished by the waves or a weathered canyon's walls are cut ever-deeper. Sometimes when a person has fallen, even if they have gotten to safety, their scarf or a newspaper or some other gossamer personal effect they were clutching is shown orphaned and lofted away by the winds, disappearing from sight, or perhaps we are shown a leaf ferried along the surface of the rushing river, to demonstrate the trajectory the person might have taken had their fall

continued, how a person that seemed so solid and capable of movement and action can really be just a flimsy, fragile bit of flotsam or jetsam swept along by air or water.

You fell a lot: the most famous fall, to your death, off the campanula at the very end of *The Hanging Gardens*. Earlier in that same film, you jumped from a bridge into water, but that was just to get attention, and you earnestly and with enjoyment swooned into the arms of Winston Prince. At other times, in other films, there were waterfalls, skyscrapers, historic oceangoing vessels, rope bridges spanning rainforest peaks. You have fallen from heights and horses and high-heels; you have been pushed, and have jumped, and have simply slipped or misjudged the terrain in your haste to escape your pursuer. Your landings have all been elegant, cleverly concealed, or completely artificial in the service of aesthetics and logistics: you were in fact during your fall from the campanula really a rubber dummy (Roger Boorman making certain you heard him quipping he couldn't tell the difference between you and it), and Boorman had the credits roll without ever pulling back in for a close-up to show how that fall really ended, though now you are really curious how that fall would have been, had it been really a live human body meeting the surface of the tiled courtyard with the force of one hundred ten pounds plus the momentum gained from ten stories' flight.

It must happen so fast you don't actually feel the impact; given a good height and a long fall, the body would probably fall with such rapidity that dizziness and loss of consciousness would occur sometime during the descent. That much has been speculated; you don't want to hear anything more definitively proven through laboratory analysis than that, and the last thing you want to hear about now is tests in which various animals have electrodes bored into their brains so they can be hooked up to devices that measure the degree of pain, fear, and alert consciousness they experience during a forced dive to their deaths, suffering and indignity imposed upon them in the name of human scientific inquiry, you don't want to consider just how many people there are in the world like your cousin Ted, who made finger puppets out of still-squirming mice in the back of the barn just to see if it would work, who end up wearing the white lab coat conferring status as enforcer of Reason and Authority, and getting paid and otherwise rewarded and enabled for their depravity? Perhaps even the shock and force of the jump, push, or fall itself is enough a seismic tremor to immediately dislodge consciousness from its privileged place of primary observer of events involving your body.

How a fall really precisely ends your biological life: a book says that immediate death from trauma—immediate is that which takes place within minutes; early, that which takes place within the first few hours; late, death that comes days or weeks after—is the result of either massive brain damage or exsanguination, a Catholic-sounding term for the rapid and massive loss of blood due to the injury of the heart or a major blood vessel. This is of course if you fall to a hard surface; death by falling onto or into water would be different physiologically, you cannot find any data on it, but deduce it is probably preferable aesthetically. Either way, a lot of things could go wrong, it might not work, and it could cause far more suffering than the thing that you are trying to avoid in the first place when you think of falling on purpose. And you realize, this is what happens after the credits roll: someone will be finding your body, or what's left of it, and if you can, you want to make that task easier, rather than as difficult and messy as could be for them.

2. Another one that you always hear about: after the initial pain in the arm, you probably become numb to that and then

it seems like you would feel you are becoming lighter, what seems to be the substance of you that at room temperature is gas rather than liquid or solid becomes sleepy and giddy as it effervesces out of the pores of the portion of you that is solid, while the liquid part of you, the part of you that you have focused on for this method, more slowly departs, and eventually the solid part of you becomes a cocoon or carapace that in the end will be all that is found. You could do this in the bath, to speed the flow of blood, and also to keep things as tidy as possible. You recall an etching you saw of the ideal Renaissance city: the center of the city was called its heart, and the streets, its veins and arteries. You saw this etching in Rome, where you spent a great deal of time in traffic jams in the narrow, ancient streets. You fear if the path of blood traffic is not well-planned, the exit wound ill-placed or not made sufficiently capacious, the arteries will clog, the blood will come to a standstill, and again, it could cause far more suffering than what you are trying to avoid. And how many times does it actually work compared to how many times have you seen faded little scars at the slender bit of the wrist of someone still quite alive?

As a child you'd sometimes find your thoughts meandering in a chilly dark place, a backroad near the palace of the shades, you'd wander until you got suffused with a foggy numbness out of which the only thing you could make out clearly was the idea that it would be the best possible strategy for you at that time in your life just to let the blood out of your veins; you'd then scratch a bit at the blue veins you can see through that palest thinnest skin at your wrist, but the moment the amateurish incisions warmed your flesh with a burning pain, it was like a torch was lit to guide you back closer to the land of the living, you could suddenly make out shapes in the darkness.

3. Drowsiness, then something so weary it doesn't seem possi-

ble to feel it while still awake. Your limbs are sandbags becoming soaked with water, no-one can move them now; the fluid in your eyes and mouth thickens to gel, the room grows dim, dimmer, dark. This much you remember from your heretofore only other serious attempt made with pills, which you tried on your honeymoon with Winston, after finding him with the cabana boy. That was a thoughtless act, a rash overreaction, an out-of-proportion response to the situation at hand, and it did not take long afterward for you then to be glad you had failed. Though as a younger person you had many times wished for annihilation in some form, you consider now how you experienced the happiest moments of your life since the last time you tried with any seriousness, and it is that realization that makes you feel you're all the more correct in knowing that now is, at last, the appropriate time. This book you've purchased says if you do it right you can do it with pills: the anonymous professionals who've written the book as a service to people in your situation say to have a small meal two hours before you mix the pills into yogurt which you then also consume. Despite the book's assurances you suspect your stomach is still a healthy little feral creature imprisoned in the caverns of the rest of your rotting body and it still will want to wake up everyday and be fed wholesome food, so it would probably expel the powdered capsules, spit them back at its keeper, when it recognizes it has been fed something other than nutrition.

4. The veterinary Nembutal may be difficult to obtain; it was once so readily available in the animal sanctuary's infirmary you used to visit every day, but someone perhaps saw your eyes searching the shelf the last time you stopped in, or maybe just took care to hide it all because they saw that you've got that infamous book, which recommends it highly? One six-point-five gram bottle does the job in two hours, and two bottles is almost immediately lethal, if you follow the instructions: first,

the small meal so common to most of the recommended methods, along with a dose of some antiemetics, such as taken for seasickness; then two hours later the Nembutal itself—chug it quickly, you are admonished. You are advised that with this method, any dallying means mere sleep and therefore failure, you must follow the Nembutal shot with a chaser of alcohol or juice laced with artificial sugar so the disgusting taste of the Nembutal does not cause immediate "rejection," as they put it.

5. This method is described in the book as lacking in aesthetics but making up for it in efficacy. You are advised first to "don a paper painter's mask"—what on earth does a "paper painter's mask" look like? You phoned several hardware stores, and the young clerks—all the pimply summer help—put you on hold, and no-one ever took the line. Or you were asked, did you mean a respirator to protect you from fumes? Or something to keep the paint out of your face? You were told, yes, we have one of those, then, click, connection ended. You would like to know what it looks like beforehand, especially as in this book you have, which so thoughtfully goes into great detail to help you find the most effective method involving the least amount of suffering, you have been advised to take some time choosing the size, shape, and color of the plastic bag, to think about the appearance of the bag, to take into account that if you select a larger bag you must be willing to allow it all to happen more slowly, you learn, because the carbon dioxide takes longer to accumulate and the oxygen takes longer to be consumed from the larger space; though they tell you to take the entire appearance of the bag into account, and explain that the size influences the timing of the event, they do not ever explain what difference the shape or color makes.

So, the instructions say: 1. Don a paper painter's mask. "Don," such a merry verb they use. Don we now our grim apparel: the paper painter's mask somehow keeps the plastic bag, which is put on over it, from being sucked into the mouth and nostrils—and, of course, you have already ingested the by-now familiar small meal, and then the capsules mixed into yogurt—oh, it's getting difficult to keep the instructions straight, repeat from the top: eat a small meal, then an hour or so later, take your sleeping pills mixed into yogurt, then put on the paper painter's mask, and over that put the plastic bag, and over that two rubber bands over the plastic bag and around your neck which will eventually seal the bag to your skin but which first you hold away from your neck awhile as you wait for the pills to start working. You wait to fall asleep, at which time your hands will drop, letting the rubber bands seal the bag up tight against your neck; then, breathing continues as you sleep, and the whole thing, they say, actually works due to the lack of oxygen to the brain, which you are said not to miss since you are asleep—it isn't suffocation in the usual sense of the word; there is no choking, you are assured, you sleep through it all. Oh, now you notice, here they add, a slightly-reclining but mostly-upright position is necessary, so that if you fall asleep quickly, your hands simply fall to your sides and the bag closes properly—this posture reminds you of trying to sleep on an airplane, which you have never been able to do, and you wonder if this method can really work for you. You keep reading: further down in the instructions, it is also recommended that you choose a cool room, as a warm environment will exaggerate the "natural heating effect of the enclosed plastic bag." The so-called "natural heating effect" of a plastic bag enclosing one's head in an elaborate premeditated attempt to end one's life seems a poor choice of words to you, it seems a very strange idea of what "natural" might be. Nonetheless, you keep reading, only to be told that should you be bothered by the plastic bag on your forehead and eyes, which evidently the paper painter's mask does not help with, you might want to wear a hat with a stiff brim, such as a baseball cap, to keep the plastic away from your forehead.

You wonder what kind of person would be reading this book having not already, catching sight of the scissors in the drawer, the razor blade in the toolbox, the knife on its expensive magnetic strip in the remodeled kitchen, regarded each as potential weapons to wield at the wrist; having not already, searching for headache remedies for dinner guests and children, contemplated the assortment of bottles in the medicine cabinet, and coming in from the car late at night, the canisters of various –cides in the garage, as materials to ingest. You wonder what kind of person could write all these instructions in this book, conjuring the whole gestalt of you groggily succumbing to darkness with the taste of yogurt and bitter pills in your mouth, the surely ridiculous and terrifying sight of a seated body with head covered by a plastic bag, no matter what color you've chosen, rubber-banded around your neck, your silhouette ducklike from the bill of the cap protruding underneath the plastic. You are furious at a person who would suggest that you—who has already endured both searing and aching pain that the morphine is no longer quenching, who has already endured the fetid stench of your epithelial tissues rotting in every orifice, whose vital organs like liver and kidneys cannot perform their functions effectively because insufficient tissue remains free from infiltration by rapacious cells, whose hollow structures are obstructed by masses so that both nourishment and elimination are severely painful and ineffective, you who has already endured patiently reading through different scenarios involving absurd and grotesque costumes and settings, you who has obviously displayed great tenacity and focus in your pursuits even under barrage of significant obstacles and distractions—might be "bothered" by a "natural" heating effect, or the feel of plastic on your forehead and eyes, as you kill yourself by consuming large amounts of sleeping pills and suffocating yourself with a plastic bag.

And on top of it all, there are so many steps to remember, it seems very easy to go wrong somewhere, despite the reportedly high rate of efficacy for this method. You consider writing the authors a note suggesting that the instructions would be less confusing if they more closely resembled a cooking recipe, in which all needed ingredients are listed first, with hints on where to find the more unusual ingredients, followed by complete step-by-step instructions, as opposed to the casual narrative style they have chosen.

6. If only someone could tell you exactly how it feels, if you just let your impending death from cancer proceed as it wishes. It seems an act committed by a separate personality, with a mind of its own. The first physician in written history to describe cancer, Galen insisted in the year 200 that a cancer tumor resembled a crab whose legs extended outward from its body into the flesh of the unfortunate person hosting it—in this description he may have been displaying an antique hyperbole inspired by the poetry of its name, the Latin "cancer" being derived from the Greek "karkinos," which came to mean "crab," but in fact originally simply meant "hard," which the cancer as a mass is, and it is probably more hard than it is like a crab. But in other ways, it does seem an animal with, if not a mind, at least a survival instinct of its own: the cancer tumor can be removed and yet regrow itself with a vengeance in not only its original location but elsewhere in other organs and tissues. Once challenged by the knife, the cancer changes strategies; it stops being a lone hard mass and transforms into a fluid substance of swarming particles of mini-masses that swims in the channels of the body, its members insinuating themselves into any nooks or crannies in which they can get a toehold, lodging

themselves into niches in which they can hide out and steal nourishment to grow themselves—and that is what has happened to Kitty Dawson.

What would it feel like to just defer to this hunger? How bad is it, really, to be eaten, in a slow, cell-by-cell process, unlike the more commonly depicted devourings in nature involving the coarse biting and shredding of a fanged and clawed predator?

As you consider this last notion, and images of your beloved big cats to whom you have given sanctuary, who to you have given sanctuary, are brought to mind, and the storm in your head at last recedes, leaving in its wake a quiet and calm: you realize you do not have to choose the best of all possible methods, because no matter what, it will definitely occur, one way or the other, and it will happen just once, and then it will be just be over, and it will not matter any more how well you did it. And for that very fact you begin to feel a gratitude and ease you have not really felt to this degree since you wrapped what you knew at the time would be your last picture.

XII   ANIMAL SANCTUARY

Esteemed Members of the Society:

I write to you today aware that in light of recent events, many of us have matters of great
urgency to which we must attend; and so I will
keep my letter as brief as possible. To those of
you for whom condolences are in order, I ex-
tend my deepest heartfelt sympathies. I share
in your losses, grief, and anxiety.

Now is surely a time for humility, caution, fru-
gality, and individual sacrifice for the common
good; it is also my conviction that not only despite—but in fact, precisely because of—the trying, chaotic times in which we currently find
ourselves, we must take care that in allocating
limited resources to appropriate priorities, we

do not in the haste of emergencies and crises abandon too much that once lost can never be replaced; that in the face of destruction and impermanence, we still strive to maintain things worth maintaining.

Today, I humbly ask a bit of your time as I speak to you all in support of those members and staff of the Society who wish to allocate funds for the maintenance of the Society's Hall of Animals, which my grandfather Frank Atkins began planning in 1910 and which was completed in 1928.

I realize—because of many members' response to my article that was published last year, the excerpt from my still-unfinished biography of my grandfather—to some of you I may seem an unlikely ally, or a likely foe of the Society as a whole. I do not see it as such a black-and-white issue—and there are in fact some members of the Society who have individually contacted me to tell me they feel my work is very valuable. But even for those of you who strongly disagree with what I have written, I hope that in these times, we can unite where we may and ally ourselves to pursue common needs and purposes regardless of other differences of opinion we may have.

For my grandfather, the Hall of Animals was indisputably a labor of love. And when the Hall was unveiled in late 1928, less than a year after my grandfather's death, it was a sensation, a revelation to its visitors. Since 1928, as is to be expected, science and its institutions have since changed greatly, and our attitudes towards certain things have changed as well. No matter how it relates to contemporary scientific practices, I believe as an artifact, the Hall will always remain important to our understanding of animals and ourselves.

(When I was a very young girl, the Hall of Animals was a favorite place to go: all the pretty creatures! Then when I was seven, my cat died, and death became a thing I understood viscerally from touching her and feeling her stiff and seeing the light gone out of her eyes and aching with loss and longing for her warmth, and I soon made the connection that all those animals in the dioramas were also dead; dead, but magically, horrifically, never buried in the backyard with ceremony and allowed to rest, but instead forced to perform eternally and submit themselves for inspection. And I realized that all the people standing around me in the Hall gazing upon the animals either didn't notice any of this or didn't care. I stopped visiting the Hall.)

When I commenced my grandfather's biography three years ago, I hadn't visited the Hall regularly since I was a child, but I began again to visit the Hall once every week, and it has since become a ritual space in which I meditate upon my grandfather's life and work. The architectonics of the place—evocative of a cathedral's nave, apse, transept and radiating chapels—are such that my grandfather surely intended the space to produce a contemplative, dramatic, transformational experience for those who visit it. Indeed, in a 1927 letter to the president of the Society, my grandfather said of the diorama centermost in the Hall of Animals, The Great Sanctuary,

"The great ape stands vigilant and in the moment of meeting our gaze. Visitors may be looked upon by him in such a way that most of us could not otherwise do in our lifetimes and—should the animal become extinct—in such a way that no-one ever may again in his lifetime."

In his endeavors, my grandfather was interested first and foremost in what would, after he had already been espousing its central values before it had a name, become known as the conservation and preservation of wildlife. In 1922 he was truly ahead of his time when he wrote the Society,

"I am most anxious that the gorilla might be driven to extinction before science adequately knows him."

As most of you know, the building of the Hall of Animals was the focus for and culmination of all my grandfather's activities on behalf of the Society. Starting in 1909, my grandfather collected specimens and made photographs and films under the auspices of the Society, with occasional funding and accompaniment by various benefactors, most of whom assisted in collecting specimens.

(*His peers on expeditions were mostly men of great wealth and power, at a time when their wealth and power were young and still rapidly growing; their factories' chimneys and corporate headquarters' skyscrapers made thickets of cities' skylines, their railroads snaked through virgin forests, their monopolies' influence reached all the way to drawing the borders of faraway newly christened nations, their leisure time was spent pursuing vigorous activities in pristine places free from the trappings of technology-centered civilization; and their philanthropy, which they pursued with the same ardor and acuity as they did their most arduous sports, built many of the influential cultural institutions throughout the country: museums, libraries, schools.*)

My grandfather said these men, "...sought simply to commune with Nature, and preserve artifacts of it that might be displayed for the common person's edification in permanent monument and testament. For Nature teaches all: law and order, right and wrong. And Nature remedies all the ills that Man hath wrought. And if the common man cannot go to the country, then the Museum can bring Nature and its teachings to him."

My grandfather helped transition the wealthy industrialists' approach to wild animals from one of fear and aggression to one of concerned observation; he did this through adding the camera to the arsenal of the hunter, and shifting the trophy of the encounter experience from the truncated wall-mounted variety to the bodily-intact, taxidermied specimen contextualized within a diorama and accompanied by scientifically-useful mechanical reproductions. And so a group of men found the motivations for their big game hunting crystallize from the fashionable amusement of violent sport to the morally elevated purposes of science and the betterment of the common man.

The filming of wild animals had not been done much before my grandfather's attempts. It was logistically quite difficult in 1923 to take a hand-cranked camera and heavy, volatile-in-the-damp nitrate film up misty mountain slopes, but that is what my grandfather did when he made the first footage of a wild gorilla family. In his memoir he wrote:

"In terms of skill, daring, and endurance, it takes twice the man to capture with film what the gun can take. But even though I was well aware as I turned the crank of the camera that I was doing something that had not been done before, after two hundred feet of film, a lovely mother gorilla, her baby, and party began to seem a bit boring—awfully serene after the labor and difficulty involved in ascending the mountain and finding the gorillas. And I was well aware we had only another four hundred feet of film left for the entire remainder of our hunting party.

I decided to stand up, which provoked what I thought at the time to be a young male in the mother gorilla's entourage, and we delightedly captured his histrionics on the rest of our film. When we ran out of film, I shot and killed the ape, as it would be of great value to study so closely a specimen for which we also had film documentation. I was immediately deeply regretful when we at last came close to our quarry, and the young male proved to be a female in the prime of her fertility. But as it turned out, this specimen proved extremely important, perhaps ultimately contributing more in a way to the preservation of gorillas as a species than this single female could have done had she merely lived out her full reproductive years."

From the fruits of his expeditions, in addition to creating his dioramas for the Society, my grandfather's film footage from a three-year period of various expeditions was assembled into the feature film *Jungle Babies*, of which he wrote to the president of the Society in 1925,

"The camera does not lie. A film consisting of truth and beauty without hoaxes or artifice easily brings two important gifts to millions of people: first, the aesthetic and ethical influences of Nature; and second, the idea that our generation would be wise not to destroy what future generations might enjoy."

The Society's activities during the epoch in which my grandfather contributed to them, according to the Society's mission, "sought to preserve and conserve the enduring principles of Nature and her laws; in so doing, Man might benefit from her examples and, by mastering them, transcend them to ever-higher stages, toward a better future." The members of the Society during this time were a generation that proclaimed it their responsibility to "tithe of their wealth on behalf of those upon whom Fortune had not so generously bestowed her blessings," as well as to "steward the safeguarding of Man's continued progress from the lower to higher stages." Most of the Society's members at that time were also directly involved with other public and private institutions concerned with the greater good. A number of them joined forces to form the Bureau of Social Hygiene.

(Jungle Babies *presented footage of elephant, lion, zebra, giraffe, and African human babies; as in the Society's museum at the time, representations of African humans were presented alongside those of animal wildlife, as variants of the same category.* Jungle Babies *was released the same year the Society hosted the First International Conference on Eugenics, then a new, modern science. The conference sought to "educate experts and the common person as to the necessity of preserving and vitalizing Man's progress," and the Society's exhibitions were used as scientific proof of hierarchies of species, race, nationality, and gender. A spectrum from superiority to inferiority was purported to be demonstrated with the latest technological methods of the day: camera, microscope, and a Linnaean litany in the language the Romans used to administrate Pax Linearity were deployed, the results lined up in tidy glass cases. It is a noteworthy measure of the Society's influence that leading universities and state institutions sent representatives to the conference, and eminent foreign delegates were in attendance, as were members of the Committee on Immigration of the Congress: indeed, from the conference grew the first immigration restriction laws passed in our country.)*

Dear Friends and Supporters of
Valhalla Valley Animal Sanctuary:

This year's letter is a bit early; we thought we should communicate to you all in light of recent events. I would first like to say that everyone here at the Sanctuary, two-legged and four-legged, is OK, and that we all hope as much to be true for all our Friends and Supporters.

Traditionally, this annual letter has served to update you about our activities, demonstrate how funds received have been used, and describe projected needs for the year to come. Given the nature of the present times, we're guessing that many of you won't be able to make the financial contributions to which you may have already committed. While we hope that many of you will still be able to contribute something now and in the future, we'd also like to reassure you and remind you that even before Alma assumed the role of director last year, we had already begun to work towards greater self-sufficiency for our basic resources such as water, electrical power, and heat—rainwater catchment systems, and solar, wind, and solid-fuel technologies—and so we are better prepared for the current situation than we might have been. For the time being, everyone—biped or quadruped—has their basic needs met.

At this time the Sanctuary is necessarily in transition, as are we all. We must surely all be flexible in our expectations and planning. At the same time, we can and should certainly avail ourselves of familiar things as comforts. So, as we do every annual letter and quarterly newsletter, we'd like to share with you a quote. This time, we offer something from 1922, from naturalist Henry Becker, which one of us recently came across. Though written nearly a hundred years ago, it struck us as very pertinent to our present situation. Becker was controversial during his lifetime, and he experienced great difficulty in obtaining funding and institutional support; however, in recent times, his work finds itself increasingly popular, especially with students. This quote is from *Traces and Tracks*:

"Ensconced in the artifices of civilization and its institutions, man glimpses animals through the windows of his making, and sees through distorted glass: feathers and fur, teeth and claws are magnified, shrunken, and truncated by the apparatuses of camera, microscope, and binoculars. On the basis of these partial views through lenses we reckon animals incomplete compared to our own species, as little brothers and distant cousins or, worse, as underlings and slaves. But this is ignorance to measure them against us so unfairly, when they have senses we have not, are guided by lights we cannot see, live by voices we shall never hear. They are truly other nations and tribes, worthy of the respect that we might grant sovereign states. And in truth, though we may think ourselves capable of dominating and holding captive other species, we are in fact truly all captive together upon the wonderful and terrifying planet."

Though my grandfather readily killed animals himself, within the context of the attitudes and fashions of the time in which he functioned he was reform-minded, and comparatively benign. He did what he could to make killing animals less heroic, attractive; he felt that he killed animals for noble purposes, and felt that he exhibited restraint. Though today we wince at his gambit of taking wealthy white American women into the Congo for much-publicized hunts for specimens, he had hoped he would demonstrate to the macho hunters of the day that inexperienced "mere" women could kill a silverback or an elephant; and he thought he could thus perhaps staunch the considerable flow of blood being shed for fashionable sport at the time. He was indeed affected by the violence. Following a trip during which he killed a group of colobus monkeys he wrote,

"At the end of the hunting party, looking upon our cache of specimens, I could not help for a moment to shudder and imagine what a murderer must feel gazing at the bodies of a family he has exterminated, for, lying in a heap were a mix of limbs from babies to adults, and indeed, in the diorama I had planned, a family group engaged in daily activities is what I intended to present these little corpses as, for the purposes of education and the illustration of biological principles. Contemplating the motionless pile of fur, it was only the tonic of scientific ardor that could warm the chill that had seized my bones."

During the last two years of his life, following his 1926 attack by the elephant from which he soon came to realize he would never fully recover, my grandfather planned where his grave would be built: in the heart of the rainforest, on the slopes of a volcano. It was the spot where my grandfather first filmed a gorilla party, and first killed a gorilla. And it is a diorama recreation of this very same spot on the slopes of the volcano that my grandfather feverishly constructed in his last days for the Great Sanctuary—in which he ensconced a lone silverback gorilla, the Giant of Ukwesi, the last gorilla my grandfather would kill, in his postmortal posture posed so his gaze catches the viewer's gaze upon entry to this innermost chamber of the Hall. My grandfather had a death-mask cast from the Giant's corpse within hours of his death; the resulting taxidermy is extremely expressive, the Giant's eyes at once seeming both penetrating and penetrable.

My grandfather considered this diorama to be his masterpiece, and the culmination of his life's work; certainly, it was finished only shortly before his death, which he managed to put off until he could return to the slopes of the volcano. While working on the Great Sanctuary and the taxidermied Giant, he wrote in a letter to the president of the Society,

"The animal is suspended forever in a moment of life at the apex of his existence; he has transcended mortality."

The Giant of Ukwesi was the first gorilla my grandfather met head-on in very close proximity; at long last, he found himself poised to kill one of the magnificent wild creatures in what the literature of the time esteemed to be a dignified encounter, a fantasy for the hunter in which the combatants begin their fight to the death ceremonially, face to face, as if they both adhered to an ancient, noble code of the warrior. But it was not in such a stance that my grandfather killed the Giant. Minutes after their gazes met, the Giant rushed and hid himself, quivering in the dense forest screen. My grandfather, aware the Prince of Sweden was also visiting the region and had already shot fifteen great apes, was worried the animals might quickly grow much more wary of humans, that collecting might become much more difficult—and that the gorillas might go extinct before science adequately knew them—and so, with the pressures of time and scarcity breathing down his neck, it was through a layer of quaking branches that he crept and shot the Giant in the back.

My grandfather, before declaring it the place where he wanted to be buried, proposed to the colonial occupying government that the spot upon the slopes of the volcano and its environs be a place where "all the majestic wild creatures shall have perpetual sanctuary," and he successfully lobbied to have the parcel of land made into a national park. My grandfather believed in the potential for permanence, and the moral certitude of what endured. He saw what he did in the interest of permanence as resistance to decay and, in the language of his day, "decadence"—he felt he worked against the threat of extinction, the encroachment by humans upon wilderness. Though he was not in denial of his body's own physical death, and was in negotiation with it the last two years of his life, he was less savvy about the world around him. He did not foresee that war would eventually eradicate both the borders of the nation that established the park he inspired, and the very park itself; nor did he foresee that the place he'd hoped would be perpetual sanctuary would be anything but peaceful, that eventually even his own grave would be desecrated, his intended final resting place neither final nor resting; nor did he foresee that the Giant of Ukwesi, who he'd carefully preserved to the best of his ability so that he might "transcend mortality," would also face abandonment and ruin.

Of course today there are many people who never thought to question the assumed permanence of things now recently laid to waste, who did not foresee our own recent chaotic events—though on the other hand, there are some who in a manner of speaking foresaw these events, or now see them as having been completely inevitable.

The Sanctuary was founded over thirty years ago by Kitty Dawson to offer a permanent home to abandoned and abused big cats, as well as those who simply have no other home for whatever reason. We have lions from small-time circuses whose box office receipts couldn't cover sufficient meat to feed them; we have tigers saved from being slaughtered by hunters poor of shot but flush with cash in "canned hunts;" we have ocelots rescued from black market fur traders who don't even wait for the animals to die before they begin skinning them in front of their sisters and brothers.

At present, the Sanctuary houses nearly two hundred big cats and five staff, and forty volunteers assist us at various times throughout the week. We're not sure how stable any of those numbers will remain, and while we don't want to overcommit and stretch our resources too thin, we recognize that we may see an increase in the number of big cats who need somewhere safe to go, and we are trying to plan accordingly.

How many of us two-leggeds have come to the Sanctuary running from exploitation and abuse, looking for someplace safe we can call home? Kitty Dawson herself, she never spoke to any of us about anything but the cats, but we could tell she was, like most of us, more like the cats than she was like people on the outside. Here at the Sanctuary, we have men and women who were raped by their fathers, beaten by their mothers or partners, disowned for being queer; we have those who all the other children in school attacked, those who could not abide the pecking order of office society, those who just failed and could not get along in any group of people they ever found themselves in; and we are all now home. How many of us human animals find our sanctuary in other-than-human animals, learn to connect and love for the first time in their company, connect through them to other human animals?

And now that humans are increasingly being rounded up in their workplaces, places of worship and homes to be imprisoned indefinitely, abused, tortured; now that humans are increasingly arrested and shot at while trying to cross borders, hunted through the woods near the fences they try to breach, how could we not recognize an increase in the number of people who need somewhere safe to go, and plan accordingly?

Though our mission is specifically big-cat focused, at the same time, the Sanctuary as a whole is an organism-like organization, a series of interconnected systems, an ecosystem. A healthy ecosystem and all its participants swim in interdependence. A healthy animal exists in community, so at the Sanctuary, we plan and make decisions in community, and we try to be sensitive to all the microsystems within our care, that we might affect and which might affect us. For example, we do not see ourselves as separate from our surroundings, therefore, though we are big-cat focused, we care for the plants, land, water, and other animals that find themselves in our general area.

The Sanctuary is a day's walk from the nearest border; there are checkpoints on the roadways, and various stretches of fencing, and patrols through the wooded and rocky and streambed-laced territory in which the border lies. Most of the time, most of the places where people cross it without official permission of the government, the border is physically invisible, intuited, approximated; and for most of the people crossing the border in these places, the moment that would be the actual crossing of the line is not momentous, more attention is paid to the relief-filled sensation of passing out of the liminal territory in which patrols take place.

The animals that live in the territory on either side of the border certainly don't recognize the border as an important physical feature. How many times, in this nation, have bison in their grazing or wolves in their hunting been shot to death for transgressing a border they don't recognize, crossing a line on either side of which the grass tastes just as sweet and the rabbits are just as fat, but which the rancher and the park warden have agreed is the boundary at which preservation ends?

At the Sanctuary, we are entrusted to house, for everyone's safety, the big cats within appropriate enclosures. But for the most part we honor the overwhelming tendency of animal and plant biology, and the meteorological and geological movements of the natural world, to resist rigid enclosures, boundaries, and structures. Our plans and structures are inherently fluid so as to accommodate change and growth on all levels. If you think of the sway factor built into a building constructed in an earthquake zone—how even violent and sudden change can have more or less impact depending on degrees of fluidity—perhaps you can imagine how such attitudes might be more appropriate than ever in these uncertain times.

The body, the organs, the cell walls, these are all more permeable than is usually emphasized in our schooling. We sit at desks learning to privilege and police the boundaries of our briny fluid-filled sacks of skin, learning to name our individual limbs and organs while ignoring that we live in close symbi-

osis with thousands of species of bacteria without whose help we could not even digest and absorb the food we ingest, that to live we must constantly take into our bodies not just plants and animals but elemental forms of water and oxygen, and that we must expel these things after their transmutations. How, and why, are we taught that a discrete form is the principle of individuation, that a substance appearing to occupy a place to the exclusion of other substances is an individual, that a self-identifying interiority within a construct of borders that can be observed and manipulated is an entity's individuation? The pack, the herd, the swarm; the wind, a season, a storm; the forest, the moor, the desert; what circulates blood, respirates, digests; these all have individuality, though they are not substances, nor are they subjects. They are systems, they are simultaneous systems of systems of systems, each system made up of interrelated complex alliances, transactions, processes, relations of movement, capacities to affect or be affected. How, and why, have we been taught to focus our attention so much on individual discrete units, borders, and boundaries, when all that is vital from the micro to the macro levels depends upon free movement, exchange across shifting sites, a sharing of spaces and movements?

If we maintain the Hall of Animals, we are not necessarily continuing the faults and ignorances that went into making it, but if we let it fall into ruin because we are embarrassed about those faults and ignorances, are we not then also seeming to attempt to conceal that we ever had them? It seems to me if we conceal this history, we also seem to presume that we have now progressed linearly to a state of perfection that supersedes and improves upon our past—but wasn't that presumption precisely the gravest error at the heart of some of these things that now bother us the most? Out of sight, out of mind perhaps, but can we really just remove the parts of our history that make us uncomfortable, as if they were tumors that could be cut out and the rest of the body left healthy? Or is there something still ailing the body?

Lastly, I would like to point out the most literal—dead literal—reading of my grandfather's work. What can we make of the fact that the taxidermied Giant of Ukwesi was placed with the intention that he might eternally rest in a simulacrum of the earthly location in which my grandfather thought he would eventually do the same? What exactly led my grandfather to position the preserved corpse of a silverback gorilla as his veritable double, his twin, his avatar; and that this scene should be buried at the heart of an influential cultural institution? Should we destroy the evidence of these actions before we fully understand them?

I know that in light of recent events, what I write to you today is likely largely futile, perhaps even inappropriate: just considering all that I have said is a delicate, ambiguous, nonessential operation during a troubling time that seems to call for robust, definitive, and essential actions. I suppose that, though I find the origins of many of my grandfather's beliefs troubling, I am in the end asking that we carry on something of the essence of my grandfather's legacy. I wonder, as we find ourselves in conversation with violence, death, and destruction on a grand scale—perhaps even extinction—whether my grandfather was perhaps correct in his anxiety that many things might become extinct before we have knowledge of them.

We'd like to conclude by encouraging those of you who might be interested in becoming more involved with the Sanctuary in a personal, visceral, or experiential way, to do so. We are a diverse collection of humans and other animals, and we feel that what makes us a sanctuary is not our fences or equipment or staff, or that we are an enclosed space in relationship to other enclosed spaces, but simply that we are a system, united in a common purpose of sanctuary—giving and receiving and being sanctuary—and especially at this time of great need for so many, we would like to remind you that you are welcome at any time also to give and receive and be sanctuary.

Daily Herald-Telephone

VOL. 98, NO. 165   BLOOMINGTON, INDIANA   WEDNESDAY, NOVEMBER 27, 1974   3 SECTIONS, 32 PAGES

Caged lion irks Sarah

By NANCY WEAVER
H-T Staff Writer

Six-year-old Sarah Falkner walked by Stewart's Pet Shop one afternoon on her way to the park and saw a lion caged. She cried.

Sarah didn't think the cub had enough room and couldn't be happy locked up so she decided to try to find it another home.

SHE WROTE:

Dear Sir,

There is a lion in a pet shop in Bloomington. She has a very tiny cage, in the garage, and it's very smelly. The only way she can walk is with her head down.

Could you please buy her? We saw how happy your lions are. She would be happy too.

Thank you, Sarah Falkner.

SARAH WROTE this letter to Kings Island in the hope they would buy the cub at Stewart's for their Lion country Safari exhibit she had visited once.

Kings Island answered her letter Saturday, but explained the safari couldn't buy the cub since many of their female lions will have their own cubs this winter and they would have too many.

Kings Island also sent her several photographs of lions and told her other places she could write to complain about the cub's living conditions.

A SECOND GRADER at St. Charles School, Sarah

Sarah Falkner, above, has unleashed a campaign to improve living conditions for a local caged lion. She has sought a new home for the not-so-regal-living "king of beasts."

wasn't discouraged by the Kings Island response. She's considering getting together a petition to force Stewart's to move the cub to a better place.

Sarah chose Kings Island after her visit there "just because the animals were happy there."

SARAH'S MOTHER Lori explained the whole letter was Sarah's idea. She wrote it herself and asked her mother only to check her spelling and find the zip code for her.

Before she received her answer from Kings Island, Sarah had asked her mother if she could say goodbye to the cub before it left. Now she plans to go visit the cub.

Sarah said the rest of the students in her class also are worried about the cub and she hopes she can get 1,000 names in her petition.

AN INSPECTOR from the State Department of Agriculture, the animal division, visited the Stewart Shop and found no violations of state laws in the animal's living conditions.

Sarah has wanted to be a veterinarian since she was two years and drew the diagram of her clinic when she was two and a half.

SHE LIKES animals she said and "I want to help them," Sarah has stuck to her plan to become a veterinarian since she was two.

Sarah wrote the letter only after she failed to convince her parents that they could buy the cub. Her mother said they finally explained to Sarah the cub was too expensive.

Animal Sanctuary is Sarah Falkner' s first novel. A number of her short stories are part of *City of Salt* (Aperture, 2005), a collaborative work between herself, visual artists Nicholas Kahn & Richard Selesnick, and writer Erez Lieberman. Other stories have appeared in *Tatlin's Tower* and *The Styles*.

She has also written non-fiction features about sustainable living, ecological activism, community affairs, and alternative healing practices for community monthly magazines *New York Spirit* and *The Park Slope Reader*, and on US political activism and police response for *L' Offensive* (Paris).

Also available from Starcherone Books

Kenneth Bernard, *The Man in the Stretcher: previously uncollected stories*
Donald Breckenridge, *You Are Here*
Blake Butler and Lily Hoang, eds., *30 Under 30: An Anthology of Innovative Fiction by Younger Authors*
Joshua Cohen, *A Heaven of Others*
Peter Conners, ed., *PP/FF: An Anthology*
Jeffrey DeShell, *Peter: An (A)Historical Romance*
Nicolette deCsipkay, *Black Umbrella Stories*, illustrated by Francesca deCsipkay
Raymond Federman, *My Body in Nine Parts*, with photographs by Steve Murez
Raymond Federman, *Shhh: The Story of a Childhood*
Raymond Federman, *The Voice in the Closet*
Raymond Federman and George Chambers, *The Twilight of the Bums*, with cartoon accompaniment by T. Motley
Sara Greenslit, *The Blue of Her Body*
Johannes Göransson, *Dear Ra: A Story in Flinches*
Joshua Harmon, *Quinnehtukqut*
Harold Jaffe, *Beyond the Techno-Cave: A Guerrilla Writer's Guide to Post-Millennial Culture*
Stacey Levine, *The Girl with Brown Fur: stories & tales*
Janet Mitchell, *The Creepy Girl and other stories*
Alissa Nutting, *Unclean Jobs for Women and Girls*
Aimee Parkison, *Woman with Dark Horses: Stories*
Ted Pelton, *Endorsed by Jack Chapeau 2 an even greater extent*
Thaddeus Rutkowski, *Haywire*
Leslie Scalapino, *Floats Horse-Floats or Horse-Flows*
Nina Shope, *Hangings: Three Novellas*

Starcherone Books, Inc., is a 501(c)(3) non-profit whose mission is to stimulate public interest in works of innovative fiction. In addition to encouraging the growth of amateur and professional authors and their audiences, Starcherone seeks to educate the public in self-publishing and encourage the growth of other small presses. Visit us online at www.starcherone.com and the Starcherone Superfan Group on Facebook.

Starcherone Books is an independently operated imprint of Dzanc Books, distributed through Consortium Distribution and Small Press Distribution. We are a signatory to the Book Industry Treatise on Responsible Paper Use and use postconsumer recycled fiber paper in our books.